# Strike the Red

## More thrilling naval warfare with Lieutenant Oliver Anson

### David McDine

# Table of Contents

# Prologue

Red flags fluttered at the mastheads of the Channel Fleet ships gathered at the Spithead anchorage.

Across the calm waters of the Solent the great naval base of Portsmouth lay impotent. Worse, the unrest had now spread to the ships at Plymouth where, two centuries before, Drake had reputedly insisted on finishing his game of bowls before helping to see off the mighty Spanish Armada.

It was all very different now. Officers were powerless and the seamen's elected delegates called the tune.

To the downtrodden sailors whose pay had not been increased for a hundred years and who endured a poor diet, harsh punishments and lack of shore leave, this was a strike for better pay and conditions.

But, according to the rigid Articles of War, akin to holy writ on board His Majesty's ships, it was mutiny.

And at a time when Britain was at war with Revolutionary France and threatened with invasion, it plunged the nation into grave peril.

# 1 - Admiralty Orders

Placing his new bicorn hat on his head at a jaunty angle and clutching a large leather satchel under his arm, Lieutenant Oliver Anson negotiated the broad front steps of the Admiralty, and strode smartly across the cobbled courtyard where so many famous naval feet had trod before him.

Ringing in his ears were the gruff instructions he had been given by a stern-faced Scottish captain on behalf of their Lordships: 'Get yourself to Portsmouth by the fastest possible means, and guard these papers with your life!'

He had been somewhat taken aback when asked if he was armed, and had stuttered: 'Only with my sword, sir.' But a sea officer's sword was worn more as a symbol of status than a killing tool. So now, at the captain's insistence, the large satchel contained not only the papers he was to deliver to the flag officer at Portsmouth, but also a cannon-barrelled pocket pistol by John Bailey of London, powder flask and balls.

Anson had loaded it carefully and familiarised himself with it before setting off. The handgun he was used to – the regulation navy issue sea service pistol he was first offered – was just over eighteen inches from butt to business end and would not fit in the satchel. He had tried it.

His visit to the hub of the Royal Navy should have been mere routine. He had gone there to confirm his appointment to a Mediterranean-based frigate and obtain the necessary authority to take passage out there in a store-ship.

The past few months in a third-rate ship of the line on blockade duty off Brest, with its rigid routine under close scrutiny of pernickety senior officers with time on their hands, had been the most boring he had spent in the service. So now he was eagerly looking forward to the relative freedom of frigate life.

Swapping the blockade goldfish bowl for that at his father's Kentish rectory while on leave had not brought much respite either.

Being fussed over by his match-making mother and two fashion- and gossip-obsessed sisters did not appeal after the camaraderie of the wooden walls – nor did the minutiae of his father's parish business.

Oliver Anson had never been much of what he called "a God-botherer" himself, although he was fully prepared to accept the existence of some supreme power that had created the universe. Looking up at star-filled night skies at sea had convinced him of that. But his early life as the son of a churchman had left him deeply cynical about church politics.

And since joining the navy his cynicism grew each time he set foot in the rectory – particularly if his self-seeking older clergyman brother Augustine was about.

Gussie, as Anson liked to call him because he knew how much his brother's childhood nickname annoyed him now that he was a rising star in the Anglican firmament, spent more time climbing over others' backs to further his career than he did on his knees praying.

And Gussie was much in evidence at present, revelling in his forthcoming appointment as a minor canon, in reality little more than a sinecure, at Canterbury Cathedral.

After the comradeship he so much enjoyed afloat, Anson had found Gussie's preening and posturing too much to endure – hence using the need to sort out arrangements for his own new appointment as an excuse to escape the rectory's confines.

If he had not already known the lowly place of a mere lieutenant in the pecking order he had soon become aware of it when he entered that holy of naval holies – the Admiralty building off Whitehall.

Business appeared to move at the speed of a becalmed ship – at least as far as a junior officer like him was concerned. And it took a bold officer indeed to attempt to hassle the stone-hearted porters who guarded the hierarchy as assiduously as if they were shielding the King himself.

The paperwork concerning Anson's appointment and passage to the Mediterranean took what seemed aeons. And it was while kicking his heels in the infamous Admiralty waiting room, haunted in the main by depressed, unemployed, half-pay officers seeking ships, that he had been lurked by the dour captain.

He was hauled into the Scotsman's office where a check revealed that Anson was not due to sail for a fortnight or more, whereupon he was bounced with this mysterious mission.

To be "lurked" in the navy meant being discovered apparently *lurking* without gainful employment and detailed for a job for which there were no volunteers. And this was exactly how Anson viewed this assignment.

He would far sooner have stayed in town enjoying himself before sailing for the Med, but then duty was duty.

Beyond his educated guess that it must be something to do with the unrest reported among the ships lying at the Spithead anchorage, and the fact that he had been instructed to place the papers into the hands of the flag officer there and none other, he was completely in the dark about the task he had been set.

A friendly Admiralty clerk had advanced him sufficient money for the journey and advised him that a seat had been reserved on the night mail to Portsmouth.

The clerk had enquired: 'Not travelled with the mail before, sir? Then you're in for a treat. They go so fast you'll be sitting down to breakfast in Pompey come morning!'

And so Anson made his way first to the Ship and Shovel, the hostelry favoured by naval men just off Whitehall where he had spent the night, to settle his bill and arrange for the sole porter on duty – a skinny, cadaverous fellow – to carry his baggage.

Then he led the way through the early-evening bustle of home-bound shoppers and workers to Wych Street near St Clement's Church on the Strand, where he was to catch the Portsmouth coach.

Passers-by paying him any attention would have registered a tall, black-haired young man, who walked quickly but with the hint of a rolling gait resulting from many months on a constantly rocking ship maintaining station off the iron-bound coast of western Brittany.

Close observation would reveal that he also had a tendency to stoop. A decade of crashing his head on the low bulkheads of His Majesty's warships had educated him the hard way.

There was a small scatter of powder-burns beside his right eye and he had the look of someone who had seen plenty of action. But although he tried not to show it he felt less than self-assured just now.

Crowded London streets were not Anson's natural habitat and he felt acutely conscious of the obviously important cargo he was carrying and the need to hang on to it come what may.

Uniformed sea officers were not a common sight in the capital and at first every time a passer-by came close or appeared to show any interest in him he gripped the satchel even tighter. But then it occurred to him that by doing so he risked drawing further unwelcome attention to himself and tried to relax.

Wych Street lay off the Strand among a jungle of narrow alleys and passages, a maze of ramshackle old houses with projected eaves over small seedy shops selling books and prints, many of a pornographic nature judging from the cluttered window displays.

A few disreputable-looking types lurked in doorways, apparently sizing up the passers-by. Anson regretted not hiring a tougher-looking porter and it was to his considerable relief that he came upon the courtyard of the Angel Inn at the bottom of the street.

The old gabled three-storey, wooden-fronted inn was built round three sides of the cobbled courtyard with tiered galleries and a lattice-fronted attic passage above.

There was an overpowering aroma of horse and Anson noted the extensive stabling that was a necessary feature of coaching inns like this.

In response to his query an ostler lad, barely nine or ten years old, who was busily shovelling up manure, pointed to a notice announcing "Coach Office" above a door beside the tap room and Anson and his skeletal companion made for it.

Outside the coffee-cum-dining room a thin, bespectacled man of business and a portly clergyman sat chatting on a bench seat at a large wooden table with items of baggage beside them. Fellow passengers, he assumed.

Entering the office, he gave the clerk his name, handed over the money for the ticket the Admiralty had booked for him, and looked suspiciously at the copper coins he was given in change. Instead of the King's head, they had the image of a mail coach and the slogan *"Speed Regularity & Security"* on one side, and a two-necked swan symbol with *"Payable at the Mailcoach Office"* on the other.

'What's this?' he asked mischievously. 'Minting your own coinage? Take care, the King'll be after you ...'

The ticket clerk laughed. 'Bless me, you must've been a long time away at sea, sir, and haven't heard about the shortage of small change. These days it's legal to produce these here penny and ha'penny tokens to fill the gap.'

And, noting Anson's doubting look, he assured him: 'Fear not, sir. These tokens are from the Swan With Two Necks in Lad Lane, but most of the inns on the mail route will accept 'em.'

Anson shrugged. Whatever, they would be good souvenirs of his first mail coach journey and were certainly good advertisements for the service. Speed, regularity and security were just what he required to fulfil his mission.

'Looks like tonight's mail will be leavin' on time, sir,' the clerk assured him. 'But you're a mite early so you'd do well to get yourself a drink and something to eat while you can. They don't stop for no five-course dinners on the road. Nor one-course dinners, come to that!' he chuckled.

After paying off the cadaverous porter, Anson called for some ale and a meat pie, and, nodding to the two already seated there, removed his hat and took his place at the end of the table with the precious satchel on his lap.

A stocky, straggly-bearded man wearing a floppy felt hat, dark grey cloak and smoking a clay pipe appeared as if from nowhere and caught his eye. 'Navy man, is it? Off to join the mutiny, are yer?' The man smirked at his clever remark, but Anson, not amused, merely shrugged, and the newcomer went into the coach office.

While on this mission Anson had no intention of falling into conversation with unknown strangers, especially not this sinister-looking, grey-bearded cove. And he hoped the would-be comedian would not be a fellow-passenger.

Taking his pocket knife to the over-large pie, he ate enough to satisfy his modest appetite and fed the remains to a scavenging mongrel that had appeared as if by magic the minute the pot boy banged the plate down on the table.

For a while he sipped his ale and then leaned back against the wall and closed his eyes, daydreaming but retaining a firm grip on the satchel.

The sound of hooves clashing on cobbles heralded the arrival of the mail coach and he snapped back from his doze, fully alert.

The smart maroon and black rig, with distinctive post office red wheel spokes and the royal coat of arms and *"Royal Mail"* painted on the doors, was pulled by a single horse rather than the team of four he expected.

As it came to a halt the amiable-looking, ruddy-faced guard climbed down from his seat at the back and Anson got up and walked over to him.

Somewhat puzzled, he enquired: 'Only one horse?'

The guard guffawed. 'Oh no, sir. At the end of the line the coach goes orf to Millbank with just the one 'orse for checking over, cleanin', oilin' and suchlike. Now we'll hitch up the full team, load passengers and baggage, take on our new driver, collect the bags of mail from the General Post Office in Lombard Street, and then we'll hit the road. It's all go for us guards!'

Anson was impressed. He knew a well-run ship when he saw one.

Noting the officer's magpie uniform, the guard tipped his hat in salute and asked: 'I'm only with you until my oppo takes over at Liphook, but I take it you'll be bound for Portsmouth, cap'n?'

Anson nodded. 'That I am. I fear that, like yours, this outfit's a dead give-away. I must correct you, however, as I'm a mere lieutenant, ten a penny in the navy. But thank you anyway for your confidence in my future prospects ...'

The guard grinned. 'Don't mention it cap'n.'

His own smart uniform of scarlet coat set off with blue lapels and gold braid, and black top hat with gold band and a cockade, was indeed distinctive. Anson noted the man's broad shoulders, athletic look and smiley face, weathered no doubt by many a long journey atop the coach.

'It's always good to 'ave a sea orficer, or army come to that, on board, sir. Nothing like another uniform to put off any ne'er-do-wells that think they can filch 'is Majesty's mail orf one poor broken-down old guard.'

Anson could not believe that even a hardened criminal would regard this man an easy touch. He looked far from broken-down but handy and alert, and carried a blunderbuss and a pair of pistols – formidable armament intended to warn any would-be attacker not to mess with the mail.

'Happy to back you up if the need arises,' he said, 'but I hope we're in for an uneventful trip, and a fast passage.'

'Mebbe there's something faster at sea, but there's nuffink on Gawd's earth that can carry you quicker than the mail rig on a 'alf-decent road, sir. Why, we do seven or eight miles an 'our, not just in spurts, like, but over a distance. We can do ten on a good downhill stretch. Much faster and they reckon the passengers would faint, or die even!'

'So you're quicker than the stage coach men?'

'A lot faster, sir, and unlike them we stop for *nuffink* 'cept postal business.'

Anson nodded. 'Unless, of course, so-called gentlemen of the road attempt to hold us up, in which event I've no doubt you'll earn your keep.'

'That I will, sir!'

Anson was impressed by this man and reflected that he would have been a valuable asset in any ship's company, not like some of the trouble-makers that had been causing such unrest at Spithead.

There was something about the guard that the officer thought he recognised. 'Would I be correct to guess that you have served His Majesty in a *different* uniform?' he asked.

The guard smiled. 'That I 'ave, sir, as a sergeant in the good old 56th Foot at the siege of Gibraltar and suchlike.'

'Which one?'

'There's been plenty right enough,' the guard admitted, smiling. 'I was there at the end of what they call the *Great* Siege in '83 when the Spaniards tried to winkle us out of the Rock.'

'Are all the mail guards old soldiers?'

'Mostly, sir. The Royal Mail chooses to use old sweats like me as guards on account of our being 'andy with weapons and not afeared to use 'em. The name's Nat Bell by-the-by.'

Anson shook his hand and decided he could confide in this man. Glancing round to make sure no-one else could hear he explained who he was, that he was also armed and carrying important Admiralty papers that must not fall into the wrong hands.

'I'll note that, sir, and keep a special eye out, like. Between us we'd be more'n a match for an army of rogues! Any road, most ne'er-do-wells know better than to try and stick up a mail coach. Like I said, we stop for *nuffink* but Royal Mail business. No, it's during the change-overs that we need to watch out for the light-fingered gents, and that's why us guards are ordered to keep the mail-box under lock and key on pain of death.'

Anson had always been of an inquisitive nature, an attribute that had stood him in good stead when he first joined the navy as a wet-behind-the-ears midshipman.

There had been so many parts of ship, so much complicated rigging and settings of sails, and so many customs and words peculiar to the service to absorb that despite his constant questioning he had feared he would never learn it all.

So he had formed a habit of using any and every opportunity to pick up new information that might or might not be useful later. And to Anson, as a fish out of water when it came to travel ashore, this was just such an occasion.

The pair continued in easy conversation and the guard, happy to indulge an interested passenger – and promote the mail service – proudly showed Anson his official timepiece. He carried it in a leather pouch strapped to his chest, and explained that it was regulated in London to avoid the confusion that differences in local time caused. Only postmasters could unlock the case to wind or regulate it.

The mail coach, horses and driver, he said, were provided by contractors. So, as the only post office employee aboard, his job was not only to guard and distribute the mail, but also to ensure that the coach's arrival and departure times were recorded at all stages.

Not least, he had to sound his horn to warn other road-users, toll-keepers, postmasters, inn-keepers and ostlers of their approach. He explained that although it was made of brass, he and his fellow guards always referred to it, he knew not why, as their 'yard of tin.'

Bell confided with a grin: 'Some guards use a key bugle and reckon as they can play proper tunes on it, but if I tried that it'd be cruelty to the ears on account of 'ow I'm not what you might call 'xactly musical ...'

While they were talking a small crowd of sightseers had gathered to watch their departure, the mail coaches still being a relevantly new phenomenon.

Finally the team of horses was harnessed up, luggage was loaded, and the other passengers embarked. Among them now, Anson noted to his distaste, was Greybeard.

Last of all, the driver appeared from the bar-room wiping froth from his extravagant whiskers and swaggered over, pulling on his leather gauntlets.

This was clearly a man fully aware of his own importance. He was dressed in a blue jacket with flashy brass buttons, striped waistcoat, white neck scarf, brown breeches, jockey-style leather boots, layered top coat and wore a broad-rimmed black hat.

He carried his long whip like a badge of office and, like the guard's, his leathery-tanned face told the story of many a journey on top of a coach in all weathers.

As Anson made to embark, Bell muttered to him in a stage whisper: 'That's George Sturgeon, the one they call Gorgeous George. Fancies hisself a bit, but if 'e gets uppity I may 'ave to remind 'im he answers to *me*, not t'other way round!'

The coachman nodded to Anson and the guard and, clearly playing to the gallery, made a great show of checking the wheels and harness.

Bell, watching with amusement, winked at Anson and addressed the coachman: 'She's just come back from being checked over at Millbank, Georgie boy, so I 'spect all the wheels is present and correct.'

Sturgeon ignored the slight and, satisfied that all was as it should be with the rig, climbed aboard.

Anson took his place in the coach and Bell clambered up to his seat, consulted his timepiece to record their departure time, and announced: 'Right. I make it spot on seven o'clock – time to go, Georgie.'

The driver shouted: 'Let 'em go!' to the ostlers holding the horses and the coach moved forward with a fine fluid motion, thanks, Anson understood, to the great steel springs front and rear that he had noted earlier.

And as they left on the dot Nat Bell sounded a long strident blast on his yard of tin.

## 2 - An Attempted Robbery

Clattering into Portsmouth just as the town was awakening, the mail coach attracted little attention. Those who were up and about at such an hour were used to this regular arrival, so reliable that you could set your clock by it.

The mail coach would have been the object of far greater interest if the early morning traders and townspeople on their way to work had even an inkling of the papers one of its passengers carried.

Inside, Lieutenant Anson woke from a fitful doze and stretched as well as he was able. Squashed next to the portly clergyman and trying to avoid entangling legs with the spindly businessman and the sinister-looking bearded cove seated opposite had not made for a comfortable journey.

He had resisted all attempts by his fellow-passengers to engage him in conversation by feigning sleep, and from time to time actually dozing only to be jerked awake whenever the guard sounded his horn to warn tollgate keepers or postmasters of their approach.

Since leaving London the evening before only the changing of horses every ten miles or so had brought relief. These brief halts and the occasional calls from the driver for the passengers to dismount and walk up inclines to spare the horses had enabled him to ease his stiff joints. But not once did he relax his grip on the satchel.

They had passed through Kingston, Guildford, Liphook, Petersfield, Horndean and Portsea, delivering and collecting mailbags at each brief stop, but in the dark he had not registered anything particular of the coaching inns.

Even if he had, there had been scant chance of grabbing any refreshment along the way and his stomach was grumbling for food.

His last doze meant that he had missed the spectacular dawn view from Portsdown Hill of the forest of masts in Portsmouth harbour and beyond, but he would be calling on the admiral soon enough. And the satchel was still safely clutched to his chest.

At last the mail coach entered the town by the Landport Gate heralded by a blast of the post horn and drew to a halt outside the George Inn, a pistol-shot from the dockyard.

The four by now somewhat bedraggled passengers dismounted with obvious relief, stretching aching limbs and he, the clergyman and man of business looked to their luggage.

Anson noted that the driver Gorgeous George had been replaced somewhere down the line by a stocky red-haired fellow, but was surprised to see Bell unlocking the mail box.

'I thought you were being relieved at Liphook?'

'Should 'ave been, sir, but my oppo's gorn sick and we'd 'ave 'ad to lose time waiting for a replacement, so I volunteered to come all the way so long as I could rest up down 'ere for a couple of days.'

'A case of watch on, stop on, eh?'

'That's right, sir, just like you sailors in a storm I reckon.'

Ostlers and porters had sallied forth to take charge of the horses and baggage while Bell handed over the Portsmouth mails to the local Royal Mail agent who had appeared on cue.

Anson was in the process of engaging a porter for his luggage when suddenly he was shoved violently from behind and fell heavily, hitting his left knee on the cobbles and letting go of the precious satchel for the first time since he had taken charge of it at the Admiralty.

Sprawling and winded, and with a sharp stinging pain in his knee, he looked up to see his bearded fellow-passenger, knife in hand, stoop to seize the satchel.

Shouting: 'No!' he made a grab for it.

His attacker wrenched it away from him, but as he turned to run off found himself staring down the business end of a blunderbuss pointed straight at him by the Royal Mail guard, Nathaniel Bell, late of the 56th Foot.

'Come, come,' cautioned Bell, 'not about to make orf with the officer's bag, were you, Greybeard?'

Anson launched himself at the thief and snatched the satchel back. Frustrated, the would-be robber snarled and shoved his way through the small crowd that had gathered to watch the arrival of the mails, waving his knife threateningly at anyone who got in his way.

Bell had instinctively pulled the blunderbuss back to his chest and by the time he could lower it again the attacker had disappeared. In any event, Anson knew that discharging the scatter-shot weapon would have risked mowing half the gawpers down.

The clergyman who had travelled down with him helped Anson to his feet, clucking over the officer's torn and bloodied stocking where his knee had hit the cobbles. 'Dear me, dear me,' he wittered, 'I fear that was no accident. That bearded man meant to rob you and I have to confess that I had my suspicions about him from the moment he first appeared at the Angel in London ...'

Anson nodded. The clergyman had not been the only one.

'But as a Christian I told myself one should not think ill of a fellow until he proves otherwise – and I am afraid he just has—'

'Quite right, reverend.' Bell shouldered the blunderbuss and pushed his hat to the back of his head. 'I'd marked that cove's card from the start. No luggage, y'see? Always suspicious of a man what travels wivout luggage, I am. Ain't natural.'

He turned to the on-lookers and announced fiercely: 'Anyways, no-one's going to interfere with 'is Majesty's mail and passengers on *my* watch and get away wiv it, so put that in your pipes and smoke it!'

The spectators appeared suitably impressed and the guard nodded, muttering: 'No, not on *my* watch. What a bleedin' cheek!'

He eyed the precious satchel. 'There y'are, sir. Told you I'd keep me eye on that there bag for you, so no 'arm done, eh?'

Anson, still winded, gasped in a lungful of air and exhaled with relief. 'I owe you, Mister Bell. You can't know how grateful I am not to have lost this. It would have been more than my life's worth ...'

He shook Bell's hand and reached for his purse, but the guard shook his head. 'No, no, don't need no reward, sir. I'm 'appy to 'ave been of service. The King pays us well enough, and I was just doing me job. A pity I couldn't take that villain, though. He'd have swung for it, if the blunderbuss 'adn't done for him, that is.'

\*\*\*\*

Anson stowed his baggage at the George and within the hour, his injured knee roughly bandaged, was limping down to the waterfront to board a boat for the flagship.

In view of the attack on him he now reckoned it wise to stow the pocket pistol about his person, at close quarters should it be called upon.

He had been in Portsmouth before but there was something quite different about it today. He noted knots of seamen hanging around outside the pubs, drinking and joshing, many already three sheets in the wind.

There was an air of anarchy and Anson, used as he was to the rigid discipline and deference to rank of the navy in normal times, did not find it a comfortable state of affairs.

As he passed, some of the more loutish and drunken sailors, identifying him as an officer, shouted insults and challenges to fight. But Anson ignored them.

At least the boat's crew ferrying him to the flagship were evidently loyal, well-drilled and sober.

On board, he sought out the flag lieutenant, introduced himself and requested permission to hand the papers he was carrying to the admiral in person.

"Flags", as an admiral's signals officer and glorified lackey was universally known, was a supercilious hook-nosed young man, scion of some aristocratic family, and full of the importance he felt his appointment gave him.

Leaving Anson standing while he leaned back in his chair, hands clasped in front of him like a praying mantis, he explained as if addressing a feeble-minded child: 'The admiral's a busy man, don't y'know? We've got a fleet to manage, y'see? He hasn't got time to see every messenger boy who turns up waving a bunch of papers, so I'll take charge of 'em.'

He reached out his hand but, stung at being described as a messenger boy, Anson held on firmly to the satchel and gave the flag lieutenant a withering look.

'I was instructed by their lordships to hand the papers I am carrying to the admiral himself, not to any other *lesser* being, and *that* is what I will do. Kindly announce me.'

His bluff called, the flag lieutenant sniffed, rose slowly, knocked discreetly on the door of the great cabin and went in, emerging after a few moments and beckoning Anson to enter.

The Right Honourable Alexander Lord Bridport, Knight of the Bath, Admiral of the White and Vice Admiral of England, was of friendlier stock, despite his exalted station in life, and waved his visitor to a chair.

Anson noted his large nose, high forehead and snowy hair, and thought he detected a twinkle in the great man's eyes, as if he was aware that his snooty flag lieutenant had been outflanked.

'Lieutenant Anson? I gather you have been told to deliver the papers you are carrying to me in person?'

'That's correct, my lord. I have just arrived on the overnight mail, direct from the Admiralty,' Anson confirmed, opening the satchel and handing the beribboned documents over.

'Forgive me,' the admiral untied the ribbon, smoothed out the papers and began to read, acknowledging what Anson thought must be key points with nods of his head.

After a while the admiral looked up and for the first time noticed Anson's bloodied bandage. 'An accident?'

'Something of the sort, my lord. As I was disembarking from the mail coach little over an hour ago I was attacked by a fellow-passenger who tried to steal the satchel.'

The admiral was clearly shocked. 'Steal it? Good Lord! And you are of course aware of the *nature* of these documents?'

'No sir, I don't know what they are, but I realised they must be important because I was told to guard them with my life.'

'But fortunately all you had to do was lay down your *knee* for King and country, eh? Well, I can tell you that what you were carrying are the Admiralty orders confirming the King's pardon for the mutineers, signed by His Majesty himself just a couple of days ago.'

Anson was impressed. 'Is that so, sir?'

'Indeed. The gist of them had already been telegraphed, of course, but now we have chapter and verse. This tells us that the pardon extends, I quote: "*... to all such seamen and marines on board any ships of the fleet who may have been guilty of any act of mutiny, or disobedience of orders, or neglect of duty, or who have returned, or shall, upon notification of such of His Majesty's proclamation, return to the regular and ordinary discharge of their duty ...*".'

It would have been impossible to have spent the last few days in London and to have visited the Admiralty without hearing of the mutiny.

The capital had been awash with the latest rumours of the unrest. It was common knowledge, too, that the seamen had presented a list of grievances about low and irregular pay, poor provisions and treatment of the sick and wounded, and the lack of shore leave to visit their families.

But Anson was also aware that most of the demands had been met more or less immediately.

The admiral sighed. 'Basically the men got what they wanted, including a pay rise and a pardon for all mutineers, pretty well straight away—'

'So, may I enquire, sir, *er*, my lord, some of the ships are still flying red flags, so what possessed them to continue their unrest?'

'Would you believe it was what they saw as the Admiralty's failure to meet their call for better rations that provoked them! They demanded that flour should not be issued in port but that was *not* granted. They wanted freshly-baked bread instead, you see, cheeky beggars! That's what happens when you give an inch to the lower deck—'

'So, they carried on with it?'

'A bunch of hothead agitators on board *London* stirred the men up. Damned traitors! Some marines opened fire on the trouble-makers, five seamen were killed and the whole thing kicked off again. So Lord Howe was pulled out of retirement to negotiate.'

Anson knew that the victor of the naval battle against the French three years earlier and known by its date, the Glorious First of June, was loved and trusted by the seamen. They knew him, affectionately, as Black Dick.

'You served under him, I believe, my lord?'

The admiral smiled, evidently pleased that this young lieutenant was aware of his own heroic part in that great fleet action.

'I did indeed, my boy, and it's him I have to thank for my advancement, and my, er, *elevation*.' Anson knew the admiral was not only referring to his promotion but to his peerage.

'And his negotiations with the delegates have been successful?'

'Indeed they have, thank heavens. The message you have brought confirms that their Lordships have upheld Lord Howe's pledge that there will be no recrimination, but what he called "a total oblivion" of all offences perpetrated during these disturbances.'

'So all is forgiven, my lord?'

'In a word, yes. As I said, we had the news by telegraph, but some of the hotheads refused to believe it until they see it in writing, not that I imagine many of 'em can read—'

'And so these documents—?'

'They spell out the confirmatory answers that will bring the so-called mutiny to a speedy end with no further blood-letting. So once the word has spread and the men return to their ships the Channel Fleet can get to sea at last. Worth a wet, eh?'

Anson was not going to argue. A drink would go down well after the ordeal of the past twelve hours or so.

The admiral rang a small bell on his desk. A steward appeared instantly and at a signal poured two glasses of wine from a flat-bottomed ship's decanter.

When the man had left the admiral confided: 'If these papers you've brought had failed to arrive, or fallen into the wrong hands and been disposed of by the malcontents, the trouble would have undoubtedly gone on and more than likely come to a bloody conclusion.'

'So, could it have been one of the agitators who tried to steal them from me?'

The admiral looked skywards. 'Who knows? But there are plenty of trouble-makers about, without as well as within the fleet. There are plenty of would-be revolutionaries scurrying around in the shadows hell-bent on keeping the mutiny going. It could be that your attacker had followed you deliberately, maybe from the moment you stepped outside the Admiralty itself ...'

Thinking back, Anson could not dismiss the possibility.

'So, my boy, never mind Jenkins' ear, let's drink to Anson's knee!' Anson smiled at the reference to the war of 1739 caused by Spanish coastguards allegedly hacking off a British merchant captain's ear, and took a sip of wine.

Lord Bridport quizzed Anson about his next commission, and, apparently only now noticing how weary the young officer looked, said: 'You must be tired and hungry after your journey. Get my surgeon to take a look at that knee and then get yourself ashore and take a room at the Keppel's Head or the George and rest up for a couple of days. You tell me you're not due at Chatham for a fortnight, so there's no rush.'

As an afterthought, he added: 'You'll find it a lot more peaceful ashore than on board. Now that the message you brought means that this dispute is all over bar the shouting, there's much to be done to ready the fleet for sailing. We've drunk to Anson's knee, so now we'll drink to success in the war against our real enemy, the French!'

As they sipped the wine, a further thought occurred to the flag officer. 'By-the-way, are you any relation to *the* Anson?'

Everyone knew of the late Admiral Lord Anson, the great circumnavigator and reformer of the navy, and almost everyone asked the same question.

So for the umpteenth time in his naval career, Anson sighed and answered: 'I'm afraid I'm only a very distant kin to the great man, my lord, several times removed.'

\*\*\*\*

His knee now neatly bandaged, Anson was rowed ashore and, as his baggage was already at the George, he opted to take a room there and feasted hungrily on a late breakfast of bacon and eggs.

Up in his room, his head had scarcely hit the pillow before he was sound asleep, dreaming muddled dreams of rattling along in a mail coach pursued by hordes of bearded ruffians.

Nevertheless he awoke much refreshed in the early afternoon and set off for a walk around the town, limping slightly because of his injured knee. His stroll took in the Gun Wharf, busy again now that the Channel Fleet was at last preparing to sail.

It was from here, he knew, that the so-called First Fleet had sailed just a decade before with convicts bound for the new penal colony at Botany Bay, but he doubted that *that* experiment would ever amount to anything …

Conveniently located halfway along the Channel coast, Portsmouth had witnessed the sailing of many other fleets, but to do battle, and with its complex of navy-related buildings both here and across the water in Gosport, this was the largest industrial beehive anywhere in the world. But there was a strange absence of worker bees this day.

Sea officers were ten a penny in Portsmouth and little notice was taken of him. He noted that larger groups of seamen were joining those already gathered around the pubs and he gave them a wide berth as he made his way to one of the many tailors specialising in nautical apparel and purchased new stockings to replace the pair ruined when he was attacked.

Back at the George a few hours later he was sitting at a table outside with a pot of ale and thinking in terms of an early supper when he spotted a familiar figure hurrying past and exclaimed: 'Greybeard!' startling a couple seated nearby.

Instinctively, Anson jumped to his feet and limped after the man who had apparently not noticed him and was making his way down the High Street towards the waterfront near the Spur Redoubt where the Channel Fleet ships' boats came and went.

Keeping his distance, Anson watched as the man approached the coxswain of one of the boats and engaged him in conversation. After a minute or two the coxswain nodded and helped Greybeard aboard, steadying him when he stumbled, as if unused to boats, and seating him in the thwarts.

Anson approached in time to hear the quiet order 'Dip oars!' and, puzzled, he watched as the boat was rowed off towards the fleet lying at anchor in Spithead.

The man had not had the look nor the familiarity with boats of a right seaman. Nor would the average coxswain set off with a lone passenger unless he was an officer or someone on important business. Yet Greybeard had been accepted immediately and without question. It had been as if he, rather than the experienced coxswain, had called the shots.

It was a mystery, but there was nothing Anson could do about it now.

And as he made his way slowly back to the George, it was clear that confirmation of the royal pardon had now become widely known. There was much flag-waving and ships' bands were playing patriotic naval songs, *Heart of Oak*, *Rule Britannia*, *Britons Strike Home* – and *God Save the King*.

A fellow officer he met told him that Lord Howe had reappeared and ships' crews were saluting him by manning the yards, waving their hats as he was rowed through the fleet.

Already the streets were thronged with excited seamen and landsmen alike, and there was little doubt this was going to be a night of rejoicing and carousing.

Not, thought Anson, the kind of celebrations that he would wish to join. No, for him it would be a quick supper and an early night.

# 3 - Another Mission

After two days of rest and good food, Anson's knee was healing well.

He was in his room contemplating how best to get himself and his baggage to Chatham, with the prospect of visiting his family home near Canterbury on the way, when a rap on the door heralded the arrival of the inn-keeper.

'Ah, landlord, what can I do for you?'

'Gennelman asking for you, sir.'

'What kind of gentleman?' Anson had visions of Greybeard reappearing to renew his attack.

'Why, sir, 'tis a naval gennelman, 'bout the same rank as yourself, if I'm not mistaken.'

Anson relaxed. Nevertheless, rather than having a stranger shown up to his room, he chose to see whoever it was in public.

'Thankee, landlord. Please offer my visitor a seat somewhere discreet, set him up with a glass of your better wine and inform him I'll be down shortly.' No doubt the wine would be of French origin, brought over by smugglers, but few other than the Revenue were concerned about that – especially those who were partial to a glass or two.

The landlord touched his forehead and went off to look after the visitor while Anson put on his jacket, pushed a comb through his hair and went downstairs.

In the snug, much to his surprise, he found the snooty flag lieutenant who had tried to faze him aboard the flagship, sitting at a table sipping a glass of wine and looking, Anson thought, ever-so-slightly sheepish.

'Flags!' Anson exclaimed cordially. 'To what do I owe the pleasure of your company? *Not* reduced to being a messenger boy running an errand, I trust?'

Ashore, and out of the protective shadow of his master, the flag lieutenant had the air of a fish embarrassed at getting hooked, and clearly wished to make amends for their first meeting.

He got straight to the point. 'Look Anson, when you came on board the flagship the other day I may have been a little—'

'Rude?' Anson queried mischievously. 'Perish the thought, Flags! I suppose the guard dog part of your role is to ensure that the admiral is not bothered with trivia?'

Not registering the canine reference and obviously relieved at the diplomatic lifeline he had been thrown, the flag lieutenant was only too happy to agree. 'Exactly! You wouldn't believe how many officers come demanding an interview and bleating about this and that …'

Anson joined his visitor at the table and the landlord poured him a glass. 'Anyway, Flags, I doubt that you came here to apologise for barking at the admiral's visitors. So perhaps you can explain why you have sought me out?'

'Yes, well, now we've put that to rest, the admiral has sent me to enlist your aid again. The, er, *problems* with the men at Spithead seem to have been resolved now that they've been told they've been pardoned and granted pretty well all they asked for …'

'I took a stroll this morning and although I had to pick my way through the comatose bodies of men who'd over-indulged while celebrating the King's pardon I didn't spot any red flags. So I take it that all's well that ends well and the fleet can weigh anchor?'

'Well, yes, but some so-called delegates from the Nore are here to find out what the score is and are whispering that a mutiny is about to begin *there*. I'd hang every damned one of them from the yardarm if I had my way, wretched agitators!'

Mention of the Nore caught Anson's attention. It was to that great anchorage in the estuaries of the Thames and Medway that he would soon be heading to rendezvous with the store-ship that was to take him to the Mediterranean to join his next ship.

'Yes, I'd hang 'em or at least flog 'em,' the flag lieutenant added vehemently, 'but the admiral's treading softly. He's giving the Nore delegates copies of the Act of Parliament acceding to the mutineers' demands – and of the pardon – and telling them to go back and convince their fellows that they are covered too.'

'So there's no occasion for the Nore fleet to mutiny?'

'Correct.'

Anson asked: 'It's obviously a matter of urgency to get the word there quickly if it's to be nipped in the bud, so why not use the telegraph? The Admiralty can communicate with Chatham direct, can it not?'

The flag lieutenant smiled superciliously. 'That's been done, of course. But we have just been warned that the Nore trouble-makers won't accept an assurance via the telegraph. They claim something that comes through the air, as it were, rather than on paper can be denied later. Damned ignorant fools!'

'So why doesn't the Admiralty send them copies direct – just as they sent me here?'

'It's not *my* admiral's place to order their Lordships about. Anyway, as far as they're concerned the authenticated copies of the actual documents have been passed to the Nore delegates who are here, and they expect *them* to take the written proof back to the Medway post haste.'

'So, why are you here and how can I help?'

'By delivering this.' The flag lieutenant produced a sealed package from an inside pocket. 'The wretched Nore delegates are currently carousing ashore, celebrating with a good many of our seamen who by rights should be on board preparing to sail. There's no way they are going to set off for Sheerness until tomorrow at the earliest, and then the journey will take them a minimum of two days.'

'So at best it will be several days before the written proof arrives in the ships at the Nore.'

'That's right, *if* they can be trusted to deliver the documents, that is, which I very much doubt.'

'Why wouldn't they?'

The flag lieutenant gave Anson a condescending look. 'Because they have a vested interest in stirring up trouble, don't y'see? We believe they *want* a mutiny. All the time they are swanning around laying the law down to their superiors, these agitators feel important – powerful. The minute things get back to normal again they will revert to being the lowlife they really are, mere dogsbodies, scrubbing decks and touching their forelocks to their betters.'

Anson sighed. 'Flags, has it ever occurred to you that one of the reasons for the mutiny is that the lower deck feel despised and worthless?'

'You'd defend them?'

Anson shook his head almost despairingly. 'Defend them? No. But I'd like to think I understand their frustration.'

The flag lieutenant was clearly unimpressed. 'Take care. Sounds as if you're close to joining them.'

Irritated, Anson snapped: 'I abhor mutiny, but before we condemn them we should look into our own hearts and ask ourselves if we could have done more to prevent this unrest.'

Shrugging, the flag lieutenant countered: 'I'm not here to talk about mollycoddling common seamen. Can we get back to the matter in hand? *This* ...' He held out the package of papers.

Taking it, Anson asked: 'Do I take it that this package contains more copies of the documents?'

'It does, but they are, shall we say, of secondary importance – you could say they are, well, your *cover* story. The most important, crucial, message you will be carrying is a letter from my admiral to the flag officer at the Nore ...'

Anson asked, a mite testily: 'And am I to know what it contains?'

The flag lieutenant raised his hands in a couldn't-care-less gesture. 'I don't see why not, as long as you undertake not to blab to anyone. It gives what details we have learned from trusted men who have talked with the delegates about the trouble planned at the Nore, lists of the trouble-makers and so on. Armed with this, Admiral Buckner should be able to nip it in the bud.'

'So if I get there first—?'

'You could help prevent mutiny breaking out there. That's why this has to be delivered by hand of officer – and to the flag officer himself. And, well, you've now got something of a track record for this sort of thing.'

Anson smiled. 'Let's hope he hasn't got too zealous a flag lieutenant guarding him!'

But the heavy irony was lost on his visitor, who continued: 'Look, you've got to get yourself to Chatham to take passage out to the Med, have you not? So this simply entails setting off earlier, this very day in fact, and handing the letter and copies of the pardon documents over at the other end. Not a problem, I should think. The admiral said it's up to you how you get there, but it must be by the fastest possible means.'

That sounded familiar. Anson nodded and took the package. Already his mind was churning over the alternatives. A sea passage, perhaps, but what if there were adverse winds? And in any event, fall-out from the mutiny could complicate travel by sea right now.

Hiring a horse and riding all the way might have worked for some, but not for a sea officer like him unused to the saddle. So it must be coach …

As the flag lieutenant got up to leave, he confided: 'Now I must get back to the flagship. We're sailing on the tide, although God knows how, with hundreds of men carousing ashore and running riot around the countryside.'

Then he remembered. 'Look, Anson, my admiral told me to impress upon you that this may or may not be a fool's errand, but he is insistent that we try it, is that clear?'

Anson nodded. It was pretty clear to him who that fool would be if this mission was unsuccessful.

The flag lieutenant paused at the door. 'Oh, one more thing, the admiral said I was to tell you that you are to guard his letter with your life.'

Anson muttered: 'Now where have I heard *that* before?'
\*\*\*\*

Alone again, Anson called for the landlord. No-one knew the ins and outs of travel better than publicans, especially those whose premises were used by the London coaches.

'Staging or taking a post-chaise across country would be slow and difficult, sir, there being no route you could call direct. No bounds how long it could take – several days at least.'

Anson shook his head. No, that would not do.

'You need to get there quicker, sir? Well, your best bet is to go back to London with the mail coach. There's a seat available tonight, you'd be in London for breakfast and with any luck you could be in Chatham by sometime tomorrow afternoon.'

It was sound advice and Anson took it.

There was time for an early supper before the mail coach was due to leave, and, having arranged for a porter to bring his luggage down and settled his bill, he was ready to go when the call went out for passengers to embark.

Outside, he nodded to the shaven-headed coachman and spun defensively at a tap on his shoulder. This time it was not Greybeard but the familiar face of the guard. 'Mister Bell! I didn't expect to see you. I thought you would have left here before now.'

'That's what should have happened, cap'n, sorry, *sir*. But as you know we don't usually do the whole stint. That was what you might call out of the ordinary when you came down the other day. Remember, I was supposed to 'ave changed over at Liphook, but my oppo was sick, so I came all the way?'

Anson nodded. 'So like me you've been here since then?'

'That's right, sir. On account of that long stint I was due a couple of rest days so I spent 'em down 'ere with a, er, *friend*, out Southsea way. But all good things come to an end and what comes down must go back up, as they say, so now I'm on my way back up the line.'

This was good news for Anson. He asked: 'Will you do the full journey again?'

'I 'ope not. It's a bit much doing that sort of distance swaying about on top of the coach in all wevvers, dealing wiv the mail and all that. No, I'm due orf at Liphook again, if my mate's fit or they can find a replacement, that is. If not, well—'

'Anyway, I'm relieved that at least I'll be starting the journey with someone I trust.'

'Thank you kindly, sir. It's a pleasure to 'ave you on board again. I 'ope you delivered your package wivout further ado?'

'I did indeed, thank you for asking. Let's hope we don't have Greybeard as a passenger this time—'

'Oh no, sir! I've marked '*is* card. If he comes across my gun-sights again I'll have him. No, there's only a counting 'ouse gent and two ladies sharing wiv you tonight, and wiv me riding blunderbuss we won't have any trouble!'

But Anson instinctively hugged the satchel containing the documents and his pistol tighter. Bell could be wrong.

\*\*\*\*

Before mounting, Anson saw his baggage on board and introduced himself to the financial gentleman, one Obadiah Pettiworth, and the two ladies, who turned out to be a pretty young thing, a Miss Wilkinson, chaperoned by her maiden aunt, confusingly *also* a Miss Wilkinson, travelling up to stay with the London branch of their family.

The short, chubby Pettiworth, sporting a large purplish nose and extravagant side-whiskers of the kind that on board ship would be called buggers' grips, confided in Anson and the ladies: 'I don't mind telling you that I'm relieved to have such a handy-looking man as guard – and to have you, sir, as a fellow-passenger. I'm quite sure a naval man knows how to handle himself in a crisis.'

The maiden aunt looked concerned at the mention of a crisis and Anson chose to lighten the mood. 'Crisis, sir? I'm confident that we won't encounter one, unless one of the horses sheds a shoe or a wheel falls off!' But as soon as the words were out of his mouth he could see that far from calming the aunt he had alarmed her even more.

'Oh dear me, is that likely to happen?' she asked, wide-eyed. 'Is it usual to lose a wheel.'

'Don't be silly, aunt!' her niece exclaimed. 'I'm sure Mister Anson meant that merely as an example of the *worst* that could happen.'

Anson returned her smile, thinking 'what a sensible girl' and confirmed: 'Exactly, Miss, er, Wilkinson. And I can assure you ladies from personal experience that *much* worse happens at sea!'

The aunt dabbed her brow with a lace handkerchief and the young Miss Wilkinson giggled, but Pettiworth was scepticall and patted the large leather bag on his lap. 'Losing a wheel's the least of my worries. There's been too many good-for-nothings hanging around Portsmouth since this confounded mutiny started. I hear some ne'er-do-well tried to rob a passenger who arrived on this very coach just a couple of days ago ...'

Anson thought it wiser not to mention that he had been the intended victim and let Pettiworth burble on.

'I don't mind telling you, sir, ladies, I'm only too glad to be getting out of Portsmouth. Just so long as I arrive in London with what's in this bag still intact and all in one piece myself I'll be happy.'

Anson thought the man ill-advised to harp on about his bag, and surely it would be better not to hint that whatever was in it had any value. But he chose not to comment and all four passengers lapsed into silence, looking out of the windows as the coach left Portsmouth via the Landport Gate and headed for London.

It was a hot and humid evening and at first uncomfortably close in the coach but it soon became more bearable as draughts from its gathering speed stirred the air.

Their journey continued without incident and with only occasional exchanges of conversation about their progress and the passing scene.

At one stage the younger Miss Wilkinson plucked up courage to ask if he had recently been to sea, and although confirming that he had, Anson was uncomfortable talking of life afloat to land-based creatures with whom he had no shared experience so he sought to deflect matters by addressing Pettiworth.

'You work in a counting house I gather, sir?'

'Work in it? I *run* it. You could say I'm the captain of it, sir!'

Anson pretended to be impressed. 'Being a simpleton regarding financial matters myself, I have little or no idea of what's done in a counting house, although I imagine it involves dealing with financial matters, tallying up money and whatnot ...'

Pettiworth looked askance at such an elementary representation of his chosen profession and asked: 'Are you familiar with Daniel Defoe, sir?'

'I have read his book about Robinson Crusoe – quite a hero to those of us who go down to the sea in ships.'

'Then you will be aware that the author has his castaway recalling that while his ink lasted he kept things what he called very *exact*, very impartially like debtor and creditor, weighing the comforts he enjoyed against the miseries he suffered, did he not?'

Anson could not recall that bit of the story but replied with a non-committal grunt.

'So, *that*, sir, is what we counting house men do for companies and for individuals: balancing money rather than comforts and miseries, though come to think on it, there can be similarities—'

'Really, sir? I am amazed!'

'Oh yes, we are the very oil without which commerce could not function efficiently ...'

Oily was a word that Anson thought he could well associate with his fellow-passenger.

'Indeed, we are not only the keepers of the financial records but are purveyors of advice to the moneyed classes regarding the wisdom of investment opportunities—'

'Allow me to observe, sir, Portsmouth is an odd place for a financial man to visit during a mutiny, is it not?'

'Ah, but that's the very point. With so many officers kicking their heels ashore wondering what on earth to do with all their prize money, it was a *perfect* time to come among them and advise them how to invest it. I'd be more than happy to oblige you, too, in that regard, sir, should you have money you wish to grow …'

Anson confessed: 'I very much regret that the little I have squirreled away would hardly keep such a creature in nuts.'

Pettiworth nodded understandingly. He knew by reputation that many sailors were profligate with their money, so gave up the idea of recruiting this young officer as a client, and settled back into his corner, smiling smugly.

Anson also sat back, recalling hearing of the "South Sea Bubble" and about many investors including prize-rich naval men who had lost all when it collapsed, and he privately wondered if it had been men like Pettiworth who advised their clients on the wisdom of *that* investment.

## 4 - An Eventful Journey

It was dark as they entered Liphook with a brief flourish of the post horn. The coach pulled up beside the Royal Anchor where there was to be a change of horses – and Gorgeous George was waiting to replace the shaven-headed coachman.

The coach door opened and Nat Bell appeared. 'There's just enough time to dismount and take a quick what they calls comfort break in the inn before we set orf again, ladies and gents. Looks like my replacement 'asn't appeared. He must still be under the wevver, so I'll be staying wiv the coach. Your baggage'll be safe.'

And, noting that Anson was still clutching the satchel, he said quietly: 'If you'd like, sir, I'll pop that bag of yours in the secure box under lock and key.'

Anson hesitated for a moment, but then nodded and handed it over. His official package would be safer there than in and around a busy coaching inn, and he reckoned he'd have no need of his pistol during a brief stop in a well-frequented place like this.

The other three passengers also availed themselves of the opportunity to dismount, but despite the guard's assurance the businessman insisted on keeping his own leather bag with him, clutching it to his chest as if it were a precious child.

Anson was grateful for the opportunity to stretch his legs. He handed the Misses Wilkinson down from the coach and accompanied them into the inn. After making use of the facilities himself he waited for them to emerge from the ladies' room and they walked back to the coach together followed by Pettiworth.

The younger Miss Wilkinson was chattering away ten to the dozen but stopped mid-sentence on hearing a strangulated cry behind them.

Anson turned and by the light of the lantern beside the entrance to the inn saw that two men were attacking the chubby businessman, who had been last to emerge and was now calling hysterically for help.

Shouting to the guard, who was busy exchanging mail bags with the local postmaster, Anson ran to Pettiworth's aid – wishing that he had not left his pistol in the satchel.

As he approached, he saw one of the assailants cosh his fellow-passenger with some sort of club and grab his leather bag while the other, who had a pigtail and the look of a sailor, spun on Anson and pointed a long-barrelled pistol at his head.

The Misses Wilkinson screamed and Anson flinched at the sound of a shot. But it was not the robber. It was the guard Nat Bell who, from his seat on top of the coach, had loosed off one of his pistols above the attackers' heads as a warning.

Bell shouted: 'Drop that bag and your weapons you blackguards and stick yer 'ands in the air. I've a blunderbuss 'ere and I'll not miss!'

The bag was dropped, but the man with the pistol raised his weapon, took deliberate aim and fired at the guard, who cried out as the ball penetrated his scarlet uniform coat. He swayed for a moment clutching his shoulder, and fell from the coach, landing heavily on the cobbles.

Horrified, Anson cursed himself for not slipping his pistol into his pocket, but remembered his sword, drew it and rushed at the attackers. For a moment they stood their ground, but with only a discharged pistol and a cosh to counter a determined-looking uniformed apparition charging at them waving a naked blade, they turned and fled into the darkness, empty-handed.

The shots and commotion brought a small crowd from the inn and the landlord sent a potboy hurrying for the constables and the local apothecary, there being no doctor living nearby.

The shocked Pettiworth, dazed from the cosh blow, burbled his thanks as he was helped to his feet and reunited with his precious leather bag, but Anson's concern was for the guard. He ran back to the coach sheathing his sword, knelt beside Nat Bell and was immensely relieved to find that he was not only alive but very much conscious – and cursing: 'That cheeky bastard's made a 'ole in me best uniform coat!'

Anson helped him up and seated him with his back to a coach wheel. The apothecary appeared and together they gently helped the wounded man remove his coat and shirt.

The wound was near his shoulder and there was blood in his hair, too, from where he had banged his head when he fell on the cobbles.

The coachman and the other passengers gathered around. 'Is he badly hurt?' asked the young Miss Wilkinson anxiously, patting his bloodied head daintily with a lace handkerchief.

Bell himself reassured her. 'Ain't much, Miss, just winged, winded, and took a bit of a knock on me 'ead. I'd know all about it if that villain had struck bone or somefink vital.'

'Thank goodness,' she gushed. 'Heaven knows what those villains would have done if Lieutenant Anson hadn't charged at them so bravely!'

'Like 'e said, Miss, worse things 'appen at sea. P'rhaps once Mister Sawbones 'ere 'as finished patching me up you gents would kindly 'elp me on wiv me jacket, chuck me back on the coach and we'll get under way. It won't do to lose too much time flappin' about here ...'

The apothecary clearly knew what he was doing, sent for a bowl of hot salted water from the inn and cleaned the wound.

Finally satisfied, he announced that the pistol ball had merely ploughed a small furrow leaving a nice clean flesh wound, bound Bell's upper arm neatly and put it in a sling.

But, he said, as he washed the blood out of the wounded man's hair, he must be rested. There was absolutely no question of him remaining on duty after having taken such a hard knock to the head, certainly not on top of a swaying coach that could easily throw him off in his dazed condition.

Pettiworth was complaining and gingerly feeling the lump on his own head where he had taken a blow from the cosh, but a quick glance satisfied the apothecary that his injury was far from mortal.

As the guard was being helped to his feet the two constables who had been combing the area returned. They reported there was no sign of the assailants and the landlord said he reckoned they were more than likely chancers passing through who had had the sense to make themselves scarce.

Anson agreed. 'From what little I saw of them I reckon they could well be seamen. The one with the pistol almost certainly was.'

The older of the constables, noting Anson's uniform, commented: 'That's very likely, sir. There's been a few of 'em through here since that mutiny of yourn.'

For a split-second Anson was tempted to dispute the implication that he was solely responsible for the Spithead troubles, but dismissed the thought with a wry grin.

The immediate danger past, the ladies clucked around the wounded guard and the ashen-faced Pettiworth.

Anson conferred with the driver and asked the postmaster how long it would take to summon a replacement guard.

'Well, sir, Nat Bell was due to be relieved here, but his replacement's still sick so he was going to have to stay on duty all the way to London. But now—'

'And there's no-one else here who could take his place?'

The postmaster scratched his head. 'I fear not, sir. Nearest one's his oppo at Guildford. I could send for him, but that'll take time, even supposing he can be found straight away.'

'How much time?'

Too long, was the short answer and, remembering the documents he carried, Anson was not prepared to hang about.

Bell protested. 'No need to send for a stand-in. Just 'elp me back up on the coach. I can do it.'

Anson asked the apothecary: 'He's really not up to it, is he?'

'Certainly not, sir. He's lost blood and taken a nasty blow to the head. I dread to think what might happen to him lurching about on top of a coach.'

'There you are, Mister Bell! There's no question of you continuing.'

'So what do you propose?' Pettiworth asked anxiously.

Anson smiled. 'The solution is simple. Bell here can take my place in the coach and I'll take over as guard myself, at least as far as Guildford. If a replacement guard is available there, that's all to the good. If not, I'll stand watch all the way.'

But both postmaster and driver were adamant that this was out of the question. Gorgeous George warned: 'Only a Royal Mail employee can act as guard, sir. It'd be against all the rules and regulations for you to take over.'

The postmaster was even more insistent. 'We'll all be in a deal of trouble if we allow you to act as guard, sir. The Royal Mail is a stickler for rules and you could get the coachman, the guard here *and* myself dismissed if we go along with what you're suggesting.'

Anson was all for arguing the toss, but remembering that the navy operated according to the Articles of War – and he supposed an organisation like the Royal Mail had its equivalent – he shrugged, accepting defeat. The last thing he wanted was to be the cause of good men like Bell being dismissed.

The guard had been listening intently. 'Look, sir, gents. I got the answer. Lash me in me dickie seat and I'll still be able to do the job. This orficer can sit up next to the driver. That way he can keep an eye on me and give me a 'and if I need it, like blowing the 'orn, jumping down with the brake shoe and that. He wouldn't 'ave to touch the sacred blinkin' mail bags.'

Anson agreed enthusiastically. 'That's right. In this case the guard will still be in charge. I'll merely be assisting him and it's probably only going to be as far as the next change-over at Guildford. No rule against that, is there?'

Pettiworth, anxious to be away lest his assailants returned, backed him up. 'Quite right, sir. No rule against that! We're with you.' And the ladies clucked their approval. Anson was now their hero and as far as they were concerned they could not be in safer hands.

Before the postmaster or driver could come up with a contrary regulation, Anson had helped Bell up to his seat on the coach and set about securing him with leather straps.

'You'd best tell me what the duties are, so I can give you a hand when needed.'

'Well, sir, there's the same stops as on the way down, only in reverse – backwards, like.'

Anson grinned. 'Not literally, I trust! Anyway, with luck we'll have the right wind behind us.'

Pettiworth, cheerful again now that they were about to get under way but still clutching his precious leather bag close to his chest, observed: 'Best not forget that old saying, sir: when a man does not know what harbour he is making for, no wind is the right wind.'

Anson had been force-fed classics as a boy by his clergyman father. 'Senecca said something of the sort, did he not?'

'Well, yes, 'twere *some* old Roman, I believe.'

'Good point well brought out, but fortunately for all of us it'll be the driver who steers, not me. All I have to do is to hang on tightly to the rigging and make sure no more ne'er-do-wells try to come on board.'

Nat Bell, settled now in his dickie seat but still looking dazed and in some pain, pursed his lips and shook his head slowly. 'There's a sight more to it than that, sir. I'll look after the mail side of fings but you can 'elp by keeping a good lookout for trouble and whenever you spot somefink in the road or when we come up to a tollgate you need to give 'em a blast on the 'orn to make 'em clear the way for us. We're exempt from tolls, y'see. There's no way *I* can raise the puff after that cheeky sod made a 'ole in me.'

Gorgeous George nodded enthusiastically. 'That's right, sir! *Nothing* is allowed to hold up His Majesty's mails – no slow-coaches, farmers' wagons, herds of sheep and suchlike. And some of them toll-keepers are right idle sods who'd sleep through a riot if you'd let 'em. They'll need a warning.'

Anson protested: 'If I'm to blow the horn I'll need a lesson. I've got this far in life without playing a musical instrument of any kind whatsoever.'

'No problem, sir. It ain't a musical instrument as such – more of a warning whatnot. Fetch it 'ere, Georgie boy, and I'll show this orficer what's what.'

The horn was duly fetched and Bell explained: 'It ain't no good just blowing into it. All you'll get is a farting noise, begging your pardon ladies …'

The ladies, clearly unused to such words of Anglo-Saxon origin, reddened and climbed hurriedly back into the coach.

Bell pulled a wry grin and continued: 'No, no, what I mean is if you just blew you'd only blow a, er, well, what I said... so what you 'ave to do is put it to your top lip, stick your tongue out a bit and kind of spit into it as if you're blowing a raspberry.'

'Right!' said Anson, taking over the horn. He blew as directed, but all he produced was a feeble flatulent sound of the kind Bell had warned him about.

'Oh *no*, sir, no,' the guard winced. 'Terrible! That won't do at all. You wouldn't wake a mouse with *that*, let alone warn a dozy tollgate keeper or alert the innkeepers and whatnot. What you 'ave to do is what-they-call *quiver* your top lip. Flutter it, like, and do the tongue out and spitting bit at the same time.'

Anson frowned, trying to coordinate his lip-quivering and raspberry-blowing, and had another go, but again only a flatulent sound emerged.

Bell grimaced. 'No, *no*, sir! That won't do neither. Look, what you got t'do is fill your lungs, like. You need lots of puff. Then pretend you're spitting somefink like a bit of 'baccy orf your tongue as you blow. Try that ...'

Anson had never smoked but thought he might be able to replicate the tobacco-spitting phase, thinking that this was a bit like gunnery drill – *swab, charge in, ram home, wads in, ram, ball* and so forth. Except that this was a case of fill lungs, flutter lip and spit ...

He breathed in deeply, put the horn to his upper lip, quivered it, exhaled sharply spitting out the imaginary speck of tobacco at the same time, and to his astonishment produced a clear, if muted, note.

Bell was delighted. 'Oh, well done indeed, sir! Now all you need to do is practise as you go along and you'll very soon sound as if you've been doing it all your life.'

'So how will I know when we're approaching a tollgate?'

The coachman tapped his nose with his whip. 'Worry not, sir. I'll let yer know in good time, right enough – *and* when we're coming up to a change-over.'

'And what do I do then?'

'You give 'em a blast on the horn, too, so's the ostlers can ready the hosses. We expect to do a change-over within minutes or we'll get behind the clock, and we've already lost a lot of time here.'

Bell nodded. 'That's right, and while George 'ere is supervising the change-over, my job is to 'and the right mailbag to the local postmaster and collect the on-going mails from 'im. Oh, and I'll 'ave to get you to see the time bill's filled in – time we arrive, time we leave and whatnot. The postmasters know what to put.'

Amused, Anson raised his eyebrows, pursed his lips and exhaled. 'Good grief! There's more to this guarding lark than meets the eye. On watch at sea all I have to do is make sure the ship doesn't hit anything and that we don't get taken by the French ...'

He paused, noticing that the coachman was becoming somewhat agitated, and asked: 'I take it we need to get under way, Mister Sturgeon?'

'That's right, sir, we've lost a lot of time messing about here and I'll not be able to make it up without flogging the hosses to death. Every minute we lose means they'll be fretting themselves all the way up the line – inn-keepers, horse teams, postmasters – all wondering what's become of us.'

'Right then! Let's up-anchor and set sail.' And Anson touched his hat to the postmaster and clambered for'ard to take station next to the driver.

He took charge of the weapons, re-loading the pistol Bell had fired. It was engraved with the maker's name, *"H W Mortimer, London, Gunmaker to His Majesty"*, and the words *"For His Majesty's Mail Coaches"* were inscribed round the end of the barrel. He admired the high quality of this and its twin, both perfectly balanced, with handsome walnut stocks, stout brass barrels and fittings.

He had placed the post horn – Nat Bell's 'yard of tin' – beside his seat. He hesitated for a moment before picking it up and putting it to his lips. His first attempt resulted in a feeble, strangulated note, but then, remembering the briefing, he filled his lungs, quivered his upper lip and spat simultaneously to produce what could almost have passed muster for a proper coach guard's blast.

A crack of Gorgeous George's whip and the fresh team of horses pulled the coach off London-bound, the inn and the small crowd that had gathered to watch the drama soon disappearing into the darkness.

\*\*\*\*

Swaying around on top of the coach, Anson imagined himself back afloat as a young midshipman clinging to the rigging in a rough sea. Steel springs or no steel springs, he felt every bump and rut in the road and rounding bends was a nightmare.

As they clattered into Guildford, Gorgeous George gestured to Anson to sound the horn.

He put it to his lips gingerly and attempted to blow it, but nothing came out. Moistening his lips, he tried again and this time a sound more like a squeak than a clarion call came forth and was lost on the wind. The coachman grimaced.

Anson shrugged, telling himself that next time he must remember to fill his lungs, quiver his upper lip and spit in unison.

Despite the lack of warning the horse-handlers were ready with the new team and the postmaster was waiting with his mailbags. As usual a small crowd of on-lookers had gathered, but there was no sign of a replacement guard.

The coachman jumped down and huddled in earnest discussion with the postmaster, no doubt, Anson supposed, telling him of the attempted robbery and explaining why a naval person was assisting the guard.

Anson noted that this was another Angel Inn and dearly wished they were already back at its namesake in London.

This hostelry was a handsome black-and-white-painted building facing on to the sloping High Street with an arched gateway above which large signs announced it as a posting house and livery stables.

He turned to ask Bell if he needed any help with the mail bags, but before he could do so the coach lurched back a foot or two, forcing him to grab his seat rail to avoid being thrown off.

There was a cry of alarm from the Misses Wilkinson within, and Nat Bell warned: 'Best jump down, sir, and put the shoe – that chained block there – under a wheel, else we'll roll 'alfway back to Portsmouth!'

Anson cursed himself. He should have thought of that. Or maybe it was the driver's responsibility? But then, as a severe Scottish first lieutenant had drilled into him when he was a wet-behind-the-ears midshipman: 'No use protesting that it's not your part of ship, laddie. If it sinks it'll *all* be your part of ship!'

He climbed down and jammed the shoe behind one of the wheels, although already the ostlers had steadied the rig and were harnessing the new team of horses.

'No replacement guard?' He asked the postmaster.

The postmaster shook his head. 'I fear not, sir. There's no-one here to take over. The new guard should have come on duty at Liphook, but I gather from the driver that the man was off sick.'

Bell shouted down: 'Not to worry. I'll stick it out all the way, as long as this orficer gives me a 'and.'

The postmaster was clearly doubtful. 'The trouble is, sir, you're not a proper guard and the regulations state—'

'My understanding is that there *is* no regulation for a situation like this. Anyway, I'm merely assisting the regular guard, who is still on board. Now, let's swap the bags, fill in this wretched time bill and we'll get under way. We're already running very late …'

The postmaster gave in, exchanged bags and checked the form, grudgingly admitting: 'I'll say this for you, sir, you're a game one right enough. There's not many as would take this lark on like you have.'

Anson flashed him a smile. 'I've got my reasons. There's something important I've got to deliver myself, and time and tide wait for no man!'

He climbed back up beside the coachman, put the horn to his top lip, spat and produced a half-decent note. The driver called out: 'Let 'em go boys!' and the coach pulled away up the sloping High Street.

****

A similar scene was enacted at Kingston. But there was still no replacement guard available, so Anson checked that Bell was still fit enough to continue and resigned himself to do the full distance.

****

It was to his great relief that they arrived back at the Angel Inn in Wych Street a little after seven o'clock in the morning. Despite everything, the coachman had managed to claw back some time. They were late, but not by much.

Like it or not, he had had to stick out the rest of the journey hanging on for dear life as the coach bucked, swayed and jolted its way towards London.

They had managed the change-over of mail bags at each stop well enough and there had been no further incidents. The local postmasters knew their business backwards and Anson had eventually managed to produce some low-key warning blasts on the yard of tin.

But by the time he disembarked he was chilled, stiff and fatigued beyond measure and left it to the ostlers to help the wounded guard and the passengers to dismount and unload the baggage.

They helped Bell to the bench where Anson had sat waiting for the down coach only a few days before, although to him that seemed like months ago.

The two ladies thanked him profusely for helping to bring them safely to town and the younger Miss Wilkinson planted a chaste kiss on his wind-reddened cheek, startling her maiden aunt with such forward behaviour.

Before scurrying off to his counting house Pettiworth tried to offer him a reward, but Anson, feeling slightly insulted, declined and suggested he might give it to the guard and driver instead, and the man was happy to oblige. This time they accepted without demur.

Nat Bell was clearly flagging from loss of blood, shock and fatigue, so Anson left the Royal Mail official who had met them to sort things out and before parting he treated the guard, driver and himself to a breakfast of pigeon pie, grilled kidneys and bacon, toast and ale.

Calling for the reckoning, he waved aside their protests and paid with the handful of coaching inn tokens he had been given in change when buying his ticket, assuring them: 'I'll not be needing these where I'm going.'

After hiring a porter to carry his bags, Anson shook the guard's hand, assuring him jokingly: 'After spending half the night clinging like grim death to the top of the coach and near freezing my vitals off, I'd not swap the deck of a ship in the fiercest action against the Frogs for your job! And how you managed, being wounded and all, I can't imagine. You're a brave man.'

Bell managed a chuckle. 'Whatever, we was lucky to 'ave you aboard, sir. There's not many as would 'ave 'ad the guts to stick it all that way like you did and I couldn't 'ave done it wivout you.'

Anson shook his head. 'Anyone would have done it. You're sure you'll be all right now?'

'Don't you worry about me, sir. I'm what they call a survivor, and the good old Royal Mail will take care of me. I'll be back a-guarding in a day or two.'

And, as Anson raised his hat and turned to walk away, the guard called out to him: 'We made a good team, didn't we, cap'n?'

Anson was touched. He looked back, smiling. 'Yes, Mister Bell, we most certainly did!'

# 5 - Mutiny at the Nore

The onward journey to Rochester via stagecoach rather than the mail was altogether more straightforward, if considerably slower and more crowded.

Anson was feeling the strain of the past week's events. It was hot and humid, his head was thumping, and in the confines of the stuffy coach he continually had to wipe perspiration from his brow.

But after the misadventures of the past few days, try as he might, he could not relax. He clutched the satchel to him as if it contained the crown jewels and hugged it all the tighter whenever a fellow passenger showed any interest in him.

How surprised would they have been, he wondered, if they had only known what it contained: the written confirmation of the royal pardon and the intelligence that he hoped would pre-empt mutiny at the Nore.

Despite his concerns, the journey was without incident and by late afternoon the coach was clattering across the bridge giving Anson fleeting views of the River Medway as it trundled into Rochester.

Disembarking at the Bull, he again hired a porter to carry his bags and made his way on foot to Chatham Dockyard.

On the way he passed many establishments that fed off the navy: chandleries, tailors, tobacconists, tattooists – and was importuned by a good many cruising whores already plying their trade, largely unsuccessfully it appeared, this early in the day.

Anson was feeling increasingly unwell, perspiring profusely and with a pounding head. By the time he got to the dockyard he was almost done in but summoned his last reserves of energy to seek passage to Sheerness. At the commissioner's office he explained that he was carrying urgent papers for Vice Admiral Buckner and was directed to HMS *Sprite*, a cutter headed for Sheerness with dispatches.

The light, clinker-built, flush-decked vessel was clearly designed for speed. She had a running bowsprit and was capable of carrying much canvas fore and aft as well as square sails on her single mast that could be set when going downwind.

Mounting ten 18-pounder carronades, she was of a type familiar to Anson, having been developed in Kentish Channel ports and favoured by smugglers and privateers owing to their speed and manoeuvrability.

The boyish lieutenant in command, Daniel Holman, took one look at the exhausted Anson and led him to his own small cabin to rest. Although living at close quarters among his crew, Holman bore the unmistakeable look of a young man isolated by the loneliness of command and was clearly happy to give passage to a fellow officer with whom he could converse on equal terms.

Learning that Anson was lately in Portsmouth, he questioned him closely and was clearly relieved to hear of the peaceful outcome to the mutiny there.

Anson asked about the mood aboard ships of the North Sea Fleet anchored at the Nore.

'There's been a lot of tension with agitators going from ship to ship, petitions and whatever, but the last I heard there was no sign of red flags and it might be that when word of the Spithead outcome spreads that'll calm things down here,' Holman ventured.

'And how are things *here*?' Anson asked.

'On board *Sprite*? There's been plenty of muttering and rumours, and a few disaffected men have run so I'm down to thirty-five, but thank heavens most are pretty steady,' Holman told him. 'As to the current state of play with the fleet, no doubt we'll find out soon enough when we get to Sheerness.'

The Great Nore anchorage at the confluence of the lower Thames estuary and the Medway was historically the main assembly point for ships from the Deptford, Woolwich and Chatham dockyards and for squadrons blockading the Dutch coast and safeguarding the Straits of Dover. It was largely protected from easterly winds by the sandbanks of the estuary and the difficulty of entering without expert pilotage was considered enough to deter any attack.

Right now there was no fleet, as such, at the Nore, Holman explained, just a large hotchpotch of ships there for provisioning, paying off, awaiting refits, or preparing to rendezvous with merchant convoys bound for the Baltic.

'Add to all those the prison hulks, guard ships, sheer hulks, store-ships and all the little minnows that serve them, and poor old Admiral Buckner has probably got the world's most unglamorous and troublesome command!'

His words were prophetic. As they neared Sheerness and he and Anson climbed the rigging to look through a glass at the ships lying in the great anchorage to the north-west, they could clearly see that all was far from well. And it was plain that Holman was right about it being a troublesome command.

Red flags were flying from many of the mastheads and Anson realised immediately that the papers he was carrying had been overtaken by events.

It was too late. There was already mutiny at the Nore.

****

Ashore in Sheerness for the first time, Anson looked around him with distaste. This was known to the navy as "Sheer Nasty", and, almost affectionately, as "the last place God made".

It was a small, seedy, garrison town largely reclaimed from tidal mudflats, its guns meant to dominate the invasion route to London and Chatham.

But as a Man of Kent, Anson knew something of its history, particularly about when the Dutch had overwhelmed its fort last century, broken the chain across the Medway, destroyed or carried off some of the Royal Navy's finest warships, and blockaded London. The diarist John Evelyn had called it "a dreadful spectacle as ever an Englishman saw, and a dishonour never to be wiped off."

And now this, a mutiny heaping more disgrace on the service Anson loved.

Wearily, and feeling very unwell, he looked around the scruffy barracks and small dockyard, some of its workers' families living in three old laundry-covered two-decker hulks on the mudflats, and eventually found a foreman who was able to tell him that the admiral had recently been rowed back from the flagship.

'Not that you can really class her as a flagship,' the man told him. 'She's being used as an emergency receiving ship and there's hundreds of pressed men on board. More like a powder keg waitin' to explode, if you ask me.'

Anson sought out the harassed admiral in the newly-built commissioner's house, explained his mission and handed him the package he had nursed all the way from Portsmouth.

It was the second time in a week that he found himself in the presence of a flag officer – not a normal experience for a lowly lieutenant. But then these were not normal times.

Admiral Charles Buckner, Anson knew, was a veteran of the Battle of the Saintes during the American Revolutionary War, a tall, gruff-speaking man in his sixties and if his hair had not been white before the recent troubles it certainly was now.

Scanning the documents, the admiral shrugged. 'Not your fault, Anson, but sadly the King's pardon and this intelligence is now useless. You've seen the red flags?'

'I have, sir, but I felt obliged to fulfil my mission – and to offer my services here if needed. I'm to take passage from here in a store-ship to join the frigate *Phryne* in the Med, but no doubt with all this trouble that's not going to happen in the foreseeable future. Heaven alone knows when I'll be able to leave.'

The admiral sighed. 'I'm very much afraid that's the truth of it. Nothing is certain any more. Everything's on hold.'

'But the, er, mutineers have been told about the pardon?'

'It was telegraphed and of course we conveyed the gist of it to them immediately. But without written proof the delegates and their so-called President Parker wouldn't or didn't want to believe that the Spithead concessions applied to all seamen. Damned cheek, not taking the word of a flag officer!'

'Who is this man Parker, sir?'

'He's a former midshipman, would you believe, broken for insubordination and quite rightly chucked out of the service.'

'So, how—?'

'Apparently he was jailed for debt, but rejoined as a quota man. A bad bargain as ever there was …'

Anson was aware that some desperate debtors took a payment to join the navy to get themselves out of jail. But it could be seen as merely swapping the debtors' prison for a floating one.

The admiral confided: 'This latest unrest appears to be of a far more political nature than the Spithead affair. It's not just about conditions of service.'

'Really, sir?'

'Yes, the damned fools are playing right into the hands of radical politicians and the French. They clearly wouldn't have been satisfied with the same concessions the Portsmouth men have accepted, and quite rightly in my view the Admiralty is refusing to accede to any further requests. The result is that in short order all ships at the Nore except my flagship and one other have joined the mutiny.'

'Seems as if they were determined to mutiny whatever you told them, sir?'

'That's about the size of it. Would you believe that I myself was threatened with a broadside by those mutinous wretches in *Inflexible*! The hellish thing is that this damned mutiny puts our blockade of the Frogs' Dutch allies in the Texel at risk.'

Anson asked: 'Admiral Duncan's ships?'

'Yes, Duncan. But now he's only *one* ship of the line to maintain the blockade and he's been reduced to bluffing by signalling to his non-existent fleet!'

Anson was shocked. 'Good grief!'

'Good grief indeed! He only managed to retain control by holding an agitator who had defied his authority over the side and threatening to let go unless the scoundrel agreed to return to duty. He's a powerful man, is Duncan, and doesn't believe in shilly-shallying. That's the way to handle these wretched rabble-rousers!'

The admiral banged his desk with his fist. 'But mark my word, these radical scoundrels are not going to get away with it!'

'Is there anything I can do, sir?'

'No. The Sheerness garrison's being reinforced by three thousand soldiers but for the time being there's not much *anyone* can do but await developments. I'm hopeful that left to stew in their own juice for long enough, cut off from the shore and without any chance of being resupplied, the mutineers'll start to fall out among themselves. It only needs one ship to haul down the red flag and return to duty and the whole shameful business will collapse like a pack of cards.'

There was nothing Anson could say, so he held his peace although his mind was in a whirl and he felt desperately weary and low-spirited. His world, the navy's world, had been turned upside down.

Noting his distress, the admiral attempted reassurance. 'Don't be too depressed about all this, my boy. If we hold our nerve I'm confident we'll win through …'

Then, ascertaining that Anson's family lived near Canterbury, he told him: 'Since there's nothing you can do for the present you may as well get yourself home for a while. Leave details with Captain Wills at Chatham of where you can be contacted and you'll be sent for if the need arises.'

As an after-thought, he asked, 'By the way, are you related to *the* Anson?'

Anson, head pounding, passed his hand over his feverish brow. 'Only *very* distantly, I'm afraid, sir.'

The admiral nodded. 'Nevertheless, you are fortunate to share *any* blood with the great man. But you look done in, my boy. My secretary will arrange for you and your baggage to be returned to Chatham in *Sprite*. Then go home and take a well-earned rest.'

It was an order that Anson was only too happy to obey.

\*\*\*\*

'You, sir!'

Homeward bound in the stagecoach, Anson struggled back from a fitful semi-nightmare, not surprisingly peopled by highwaymen and mutineers waving red flags, to focus on an elderly gentleman in the corner seat opposite who was evidently trying to attract his attention.

'Me, sir?' Anson croaked, wiping perspiration from his burning forehead.

The man – slim, white-haired and soberly dressed – looked concerned.

'Yes you, sir. Are you unwell?'

Still befuddled, Anson managed to stammer: 'Just a little tired—' before a wave of dizziness and nausea overcame him and he pitched forward in a dead faint.

## 6 - Ludden Hall

It was a clock striking seven that woke him. But was it seven in the morning, or evening? And where was he? Not at sea, that was clear. Nor was he in a coach.

After a few minutes his mind cleared enough to confirm that he was in a four-poster bed, but not at home in his father's rectory. The curtains were drawn but the daylight shining through a gap in them told him that, no, this was definitely not his bedroom.

Nor could he remember getting here, nor when.

He could remember his horror at seeing the red flags flying from the mastheads of the ships in the Nore anchorage, and delivering the warning letter to the admiral, coming back to Chatham in Lieutenant Holman's cutter and catching the stage.

But after that everything was blank. Except that he had a vague recollection of being carried into a large house, undressed and laid in this wonderfully comfortable bed, where blessed sleep had overtaken him.

Thereafter, he thought, there had been flashes of consciousness, a curiously detached feeling of observing someone soothing his fevered brow with damp cloths and helping him sip liquids.

At one stage he had come to for a few minutes to find the white-haired gentleman from the coach standing beside his bed with a plainly-dressed man he thought might be a doctor apparently earnestly discussing his condition.

Then nothing, except the impression of the occasional presence of someone ministering to him and the gradually less-fevered rest.

Until now, that was. Until the clock struck seven.

He pulled the covers back a little and was puzzled to find that he was wearing a night-shirt. Looking around, he could see that the room he was in was large but sparsely furnished with the bed, a wardrobe, chest of drawers and washstand with jug and bowl, small writing desk and chair beside the bed. A few framed antiquarian prints on the plain white walls were the sole ornament.

Apart from the loud ticking of the clock there was no other sound and it occurred to Anson that he should call out to let whoever had brought him here know that he was back in the land of the living.

But first he urgently needed to answer a call of nature, so he swung his legs over the side of the bed and tried to stand. But his head spun and he fell heavily, hitting his forehead on the bedpost on the way down.

\*\*\*\*

He came round again to find himself back in bed, his head throbbing.

Forcing his eyes open, he saw that someone was sitting in the chair and, despite his blurred vision, thought he recognised the soberly-dressed old gentleman from the coach.

'Thank heaven you are all right, young man. For a time there I thought we might have lost you!'

Anson groaned and put his hand to his head. 'I'm *not* all right. I feel like death, like I've taken a terrible beating. And I've no idea where I am, or how long I've been here ...' Even to himself, his voice sounded hoarse and feeble.

The old man nodded understandingly. 'Of course, of course. Allow me to explain, my dear fellow. You were taken ill on the coach from Chatham and when we reached my destination, Ospringe, I was met by my own carriage and brought you home.'

'Your home?' Anson asked weakly.

'Yes, you are at my home, Ludden Hall, not far from Faversham. You see, your uniform told us you were a naval officer, but no-one on the coach knew who you were. Clearly you needed medical attention, so I brought you here and sent for our local doctor. He said you had some sort of virulent fever brought on by total exhaustion and ordered complete bed rest ...'

Anson nodded. 'So, how long have I been here?'

The old man smiled. 'Let me see, it's been six days now—'

'Six *days*? Good grief!' Anson was astonished. He tried to sit up but the effort was too much and he sank back on the pillows.

'Yes, and much of the time you have been dead to the world. But now the fever seems to have burned itself out and, despite your argument with the bedpost, with God's providence you will soon recover your strength. You are young, after all, and you have been well nursed by Emily.'

Anson blushed to think that some female had been seeing to his every basic need for the best part of a week. Was it one of the two pretty young maids he had noticed peeping round the door simpering at him behind the old gentleman's back? Or perhaps he had a daughter?

'I must thank this, er, Emily. Is she, perhaps, your wife, your daughter, or one of your maids?'

'Good heavens, no! I am *un*married. My niece Cassandra lives with me, although she is away at present, visiting her cousins. Our maids are, well, rather young, in their early teens. It wouldn't have been proper for them to have nursed you, much though they wanted to do so. No, that would not have been proper, so I called on the services of Emily, from the village.'

Anson wondered what this angel of mercy might be like, and was soon to find out.

His host explained: 'You have only been taking liquids, a little nourishing soup and so on, so you are very weak, hence your fall when you tried to get out of bed. Ah, here's Emily with Doctor Hawkins ...'

Anson had envisaged a ministering angel, but was startled to see that his nurse was in fact a large middle-aged lady with work-coarsened hands and a noticeable moustache.

The doctor confirmed that there were no longer any signs of fever, examined the egg-sized lump on Anson's forehead, tutted, sent a maid for a cold compress and announced that the patient would live.

His host saw the doctor out and returned to announce: 'Now, Emily here is patiently waiting to give you a bed bath, so I will leave you in her very capable hands.'

Anson made to protest: 'I'd rather, er—'

'No arguments, my boy, Doctor Hawkins said it will make you feel ten times better ...'

Emily nodded in agreement and Anson could see that it was a battle he could not win.

As his host left the room Anson looked up apprehensively to see Emily rolling up her sleeves, favouring him with a gap-toothed grin and assuring him: 'No need to feel shy, young sir. I've had two 'usbands, brung up five boys, *and* I lay out the dead in this parish, so you don't 'ave anything I 'aven't seen a 'undred times before.'

\*\*\*\*

Her ministrations completed, Emily left Anson to rest, comfortable except for the lingering pounding in his head from his battle with the bedpost.

Eyes closed, he let his mind wander over the events of the past few weeks until he fell again into a deep sleep.

Overnight he emerged partially from his semi-comatose state only occasionally, conscious of the burly but kindly Emily tending him, drifting off again into confused nightmares of grappling with a grey-bearded villain atop a lurching coach and trying to deliver vital messages but being unable to find his way.

He awoke in daylight to find the doctor at his bedside examining the lump on his head. Seeing that his patient was now awake, he pronounced: 'The swelling is much reduced and there is now no evidence whatsoever of fever. You are lucky to have been born with a thick skull, young man.'

Anson croaked: 'It's been said by some of my naval superiors that I am inclined to be somewhat thick, so I'm not sure if that is a compliment or not, doctor …'

'In this context it is. In your weakened state such a blow could have proved fatal to someone with a thin skull.'

The old gentleman entered and asked: 'How is the patient, doctor?'

'Much improved, I am pleased to report. But, I should warn you, he is in a much-weakened state. He has lost a good deal of weight and now that the fever has passed he needs a strengthening diet. Beefsteaks, chicken and vegetables are prescribed and on no account is he to attempt to get out of bed unaided.'

When the doctor had left, Anson tackled his saviour. 'I am greatly embarrassed, sir, that I do not even know your name, nor you mine I presume …'

'I am Josiah Parkin, pleased to be of service to you. And you, sir? We found nothing on you to reveal your name or where you were heading.'

'My name is Anson, and as you will have deduced from my uniform I am a lieutenant in the navy.'

'Anson? Merciful heavens! Are you related to …?'

This was the question Anson was always asked. 'To the great circumnavigator? No, sir. Only very distantly—'

'No, no, I mean the *Reverend* Anson, rector of Hardres-with-Farthingham.'

'Indeed I am, sir. His middle son, Oliver.'

'The Lord be praised, here you were all this time and if only I had known I would have sent for your father, whom I know very well indeed as a fellow antiquarian. I must write to inform him you are here and of your illness. Your people must be very worried that you have not arrived home.'

'Not at all, sir. No-one knew I was coming. It was a, shall we say, spur-of-the-moment thing, so I had no time to inform them.'

'Well, I will soon put that to rights. I will write to your father this minute.'

Anson held up his hand. 'As I said, sir, my family are unaware that I was on my way home and I would sooner not alert them now.'

'Why not, pray?'

'Well, sir, I was on my way home for a few days' rest before a summons I'm expecting to return to Chatham for ...' He hesitated: '... for duty in connection with the, er *disobedience* the navy is experiencing there.'

The old gentleman smiled. 'You mean the mutiny? No need to use a euphemism, my boy. A spade is a spade and *disobedience* in the fleet is mutiny, is it not?'

Anson could not argue. 'So I take it news of the, er, *mutiny* has spread?'

'It has indeed. The news-sheets are full of it and being so near Chatham it's on everyone's lips hereabouts.'

Anson sighed. 'So, sir, do you have any information about the latest situation?'

'Only that the red flags are still flying and the hotheads are threatening to blockade London, but it's rumoured that may be a step too far for some and there's said to be muttering against it in many of the ships.'

Anson thought for a moment. 'If that is the case a message could come for me from Chatham at any time, but the navy will assume I am at home—'

'Then our course is clear, young man,' said Parkin, evidently pleased with his nautical metaphor. 'You must write, or dictate if you are as yet unable to wield a pen, to let the navy know that you can be contacted here, and not at your home.'

The thought of wielding anything at the moment was beyond Anson. 'I should be greatly obliged to you if you would write it to my dictation, sir, and arrange for it to be sent to Chatham at the earliest opportunity.'

'It shall be done immediately and I will ensure that it's forwarded by the very next coach.'

And so, brushing aside the old gentleman's mild protestations at the mention of his hospitality, Anson dictated a note to Captain Wills:

*"Having been taken ill on my way home following my call on you at Chatham on Tuesday of last week, I am now almost fully restored to health having been most kindly looked after by Mister Josiah Parkin at Ludden Hall near Faversham, where the summons for my return to duty should be directed.*

*I am, Sir, your obedient servant ..."*

Parkin looked up from the writing table and gave Anson a quizzical look and commented amiably: 'You realise that not only have you given me an undeserved mention in your despatch, but you have imparted virtually no information to your superiors, and, what's more, you have told a deliberate lie!'

Anson guessed what was coming.

'You are by no means almost fully restored to health. Far from it ...'

'But you see, with the excellent treatment I am getting here, by the time this message has been received and a reply sent I am confident I *will* be as fit as a flea.'

'Hmm.' Parkin was clearly far from convinced.

## 7 - HMS *Euphemus*

All was quiet on board the 64-gun third rate ship of the line HMS *Euphemus* lying at anchor among the mutinous fleet congregated in the Great Nore anchorage.

Most of the ship's company were sleeping below and there was not a single officer on board. They had all been banished ashore when the red flags were hoisted.

Each ship had elected delegates, but the *Euphemus* representatives were not on board. They had left by boat in the afternoon for a meeting in the *Sandwich* with Richard Parker, the charismatic but insubordinate former midshipman selected by his fellows to be the so-called President of the Committee of Delegates.

He was the man chosen by the men to present their list of grievances to the flag officer, but now many of the less radical men feared escalation and were wavering.

With the main agitators temporarily out of the way, a select band of level-headed men gathered in the great cabin of *Euphemus*, until recently the hallowed preserve of the captain, now kicking his heels ashore with the rest of the officers.

The men entering now had two things in common: they were the ship's key warrant and petty officers; and not one of them had been in favour of raising the red flag. But they had been swept aside by the tidal wave of mutiny that had engulfed the Nore fleet – and now they wanted to put an end to it.

Called together by the bull-necked boatswain, Bert Rook, they included his two trusted mates, George Jebb, a tough Liverpudlian, and Joseph Kelly, a Newfoundlander of Irish descent who had fished for cod on the Grand Banks before volunteering for the Royal Navy largely because of his dislike of the French.

Both petty officers were feared for their ruthless dedication to ensuring that the men "perform their duty with alacrity and without noise and confusion" as the Admiralty required. This they achieved through their piped calls and loud, hectoring voices, by "starting" slow seamen with a whack from the spliced rope's end they carried almost as a badge of office – and, when required, wielding the cat-o'-nine-tails at floggings.

The master, responsible for the navigation of the ship, and who as the senior warrant officer might have been expected to summon rather than be summoned, was a reluctant attender. William Sadler, a gawky man with weathered face and stick-out ears, had entered from the merchant service and although competent at pilotage he was inclined to be over-cautious – and was no leader. He had melted into the background when the ship's rabble-rousers joined the firebrands throughout the fleet and forced their officers ashore, and he was no keener to stick his neck out now. But if it was decided to try and take the ship in, the how and wherefore would be down to him.

Altogether a different kettle of fish was the master-at-arms, Jemmy Askew, a Lancashire man who had previously served in the marines, experience that had fitted him well for his disciplinary role and for teaching the men the use of small arms and muskets.

And Sergeant Josh Kennard, of the marines, a Plymouth man brought up in the school of hard knocks, was equally dependable.

Robert Hogg, the acting gunner, and Patrick Connor, the carpenter, representing the artificers, made up the quorum.

All had been forced to keep a low profile when mutiny swept through the fleet like a forest fire, but now that the flames had died down and all but the most fervent were having second thoughts, these men had come together to attempt to save the day.

They stood around, ill at ease in this inner sanctum. But Rook had no such qualms. He plonked himself down in the captain's chair, tapped the table and announced: 'Now gents, let's get to it! We ain't got no agenda, but if we had it'd start with election of a chairman, right?'

There were nods of agreement and the rest took their seats around the table.

'So,' he demanded, 'any nominations?'

His two mates seated either side of him remained expressionless and Rook broke the silence by cracking his knuckles. No-one was going to argue with this trio.

'Well?'

Askew raised a hand. 'How about you yourself, bosun?'

'Me?' Rook affected surprise.

'Yeah, well, you've called the meeting. You've got what you might call the backing …' He indicated the two stony-faced boatswain's mates, '… and, well, I reckon you know how the rest of us feel.'

The bosun shrugged. 'What about you, master? You're the senior man.'

Alarmed, Sadler shook his head. 'Oh no, not me! I'm for a peaceful life, I am. I'd be on a lea shore in a job like this.'

The others looked relieved. It was clear that none of them would have trusted him to lead at such a critical moment.

'No other takers? You Josh, or you Jemmy?'

They shook their heads, if a little less vigorously than Sadler.

'Very well, then, so I'll consider myself elected …'

They murmured their assent.

'Right, then let's get on.'

The rest settled back in their chairs, relieved that someone like him was prepared to take the lead.

'Look gents, it's like this. We know from those delegates who came on board today to take ours off to meet with Parker that the ring-leaders now want to blockade London to force their demands—'

Askew interjected: 'And some of the right agitators are urging their shipmates to defect to France. It's not what they struck for …'

There was muttered agreement around the table. Enthusiasm for the mutiny had clearly waned. Here, on board *Euphemus*, as in certain other ships, the enormity of what they were now involved in was beginning to strike home.

Rook paused, taking stock of the mood, before continuing: 'I've been talking, informal-like, to the men. Seems to me many of 'em have come to understand that everything's changed. Most were up for trying to get better conditions, but now—'

'Yeah, most were all for trying for better pay and all that,' Connor ventured. 'But I reckon it's gone too far with this talk of blockading London. And all these rumours about deserting to the enemy, well, that just ain't on, is it?'

The bosun nodded vigorously. 'That's right, Chippy. If one or the other – or both – happens, there'll be no going back. And the feeling's spreading among the men that anything like that could only end in defeat. The government *couldn't* let us win.'

Connor stated the obvious. 'So we'd have to surrender—'

'That's right,' Askew agreed. 'And that would mean the noose for those as have played an active part in all this.'

'Or it'd mean deserting and exile among the Frogs, scoffing snails for the rest of our days!'

Hogg's comment was met with a restrained laugh from the rest, but his point was well made, and they sat for a moment contemplating the gravity of the situation.

Rook broke the silence. 'Well, I for one ain't prepared to fight my own country, no more than I'd desert to the enemy. I didn't get to be bosun of one of His Majesty's war canoes by acting the traitor and I sure as eggs ain't going to start now!'

'I'm with you there, Bert,' Askew agreed. 'Anyways, I've got a wife and kids in Chatham and there's no way I'm going to abandon them. I didn't want to go along with this mutiny lark in the first place and now I want out of it afore it's too late.'

The others joined in, agreeing to his sentiments, and Rook let them rattle on for a while before banging the table for silence.

'Gents, what I'm hearing is what I've been hearing all day from the men. At first there was muttering and now they're openly talking like us, with wiser heads convincing all but the out-and-out hotheads that the only way to save us all from disaster is to take the ship in, voluntarily-like, and declare for King George.'

'But how – and where?'

'Under cover of darkness, to Sheerness, or, better still, the dockyard at Chatham.'

The master spoke for the first time. 'But we must take care,' he warned. 'It'd be no use simply lowering the red flag and sailing away in broad daylight. That'd be sure to bring the fire of the rest of the ships down upon us.'

'And we don't know how we'll be received if we do take her in,' Sergeant Kennard warned. 'They've been setting up shore batteries and there's been loads more soldiers brought in, cavalry and whatnot. What if they fire on us when we take her in? What'd we do then, caught between two fires?'

Rook held up his hands. 'Gents, you're right. So this is what we've got to do. While it's still dark we'll send a boat ashore, secretly like, and ask for a meeting with the admiral. We'll explain how we're fixed and get a guarantee that when we strike the red flag and take the ship in wearing the royal ensign they'll not fire on us, and we'll get his promise that we'll all be pardoned for abandoning the mutiny.'

'How can we be sure they'll keep their word?'

'Because we'll ask the admiral to send an officer back with us, as a guarantee, like. Not one of our own lot but someone neutral as we can trust.'

'That's all very well, but the minute we slip from here the nearest ships will smoke what we're about and they'll fire on us for sure,' Sadler pointed out.

Rook shook his head. 'Not necessarily. We'd slip under cover of darkness so they might not wake up to what's happening until we're out of range, and in any case their gun crews would think long and hard before firing on fellow seamen.'

'You might be right, but we don't know for sure. More'n likely that President Parker would be forced by the extremists and the rest of the delegates to make an example of us to encourage the others to keep the mutiny alive—'

'That's right. And he'd *order* the other ships to fire on us!'

'That's as may be, but we can't leave the mutiny *and* sit here without a red flag flying. We've got to take her in – and that means sending a boat in first to find out how we'll be received.'

He looked around the table. 'I'll go myself. So who's up for coming with me?'

They settled that Hogg and Connor and a few volunteer oarsmen from among the most reliable seamen would accompany him, leaving the others to arm themselves and maintain order on board, clapping dissenters in irons if necessary.

And so, in the early hours, a boat was lowered and seven men climbed down the side of the ship. Their leader, Rook, took the tiller, whispered 'dip oars' and the rowers pulled away as silently as possible.

Tucked in the bosun's shirt was a message to the flag officer – in case they were unable to get a meeting with him – announcing that the majority of the ship's company wished to leave the mutiny, and asking: 'How will we be received if we bring the ship in?'

# 8 - Duty Calls

After what seemed like an age confined to his bed, Anson was at last up and about, taking short walks in the grounds of Ludden Hall with Josiah Parkin.

The old gentleman was clearly of comfortable independent means and Anson was eventually able to coax him into revealing something of his background.

'I had what many would consider the good fortune to be born into a Kentish banking family. It was a foregone conclusion that I would enter the profession after university and the Grand Tour, although the business never attracted me.'

The Grand Tour explained the pictures of Roman ruins, the ancient damaged statues and display cases of coins that adorned the hall and library, but not the detailed anatomical drawings and stuffed creatures in glass cases.

Anson asked: 'But you joined the bank nevertheless?'

Parkin nodded ruefully. 'I did. It was the least I could do after the privileged education the family bank had given me.'

Anson thought of the richly furnished house, the beautifully kept grounds and the immaculate carriage and pair. 'And you were clearly successful in the banking business?'

'Moderately so, but it was not a profession I enjoyed. We would willingly lend money to those who didn't need it but withheld it from those who did, or we would lend it grudgingly and charge them high interest.'

'I suppose that's the nature of the business.'

Parkin frowned as if the memory pained him. 'I tried to conduct it with humanity, but yes, banking is a curious and rather unsavoury occupation. I'd sooner consort with my rats.'

'Rats!' Anson did a double-take.

The old man smiled. 'Deceased, of course, ready for dissecting ... I am, you see, something of a natural historian too.'

'And you are clearly happy to have left banking behind?'

'There are worse professions, of course – the law, for example. Some lawyers I have had to deal with are among the biggest crooks un-hung. In knowing the ins and outs of the law they understand how best to work it to their own advantage, squirming and wriggling through it without rendering themselves liable to punishment for circumnavigating it.'

Anson laughed. 'You clearly don't rate banking *or* the law very highly I see.'

'You could say that. It was a great relief when a few years back I handed over control of the family bank to some rather disagreeable second cousins. You see, I was always more interested in natural history and antiquarian pursuits than in pounds, shillings and pence. Your family, of course, is engaged in far more worthy and honourable professions.'

'The church and the navy?' Anson looked doubtful. 'I would like to think that the navy is, but I sometimes wonder if the same is true of some clergy. They may espouse the sentiments of the sermon on the mount and suchlike, yet live privileged lives off the fat of the land while some of their flocks endure hardship.'

Parkin raised his eyebrows. 'You cannot mean members of your own family?'

'I am very much afraid I do. My father is an upright man but enjoys an extremely comfortable living, a good table, fine wines, hunting and so forth. But as for my brother Gussie, why, I sometimes feel he borders on the Pharisee—'

'One who uses his church office merely to advance himself?'

'I fear so.' Anxious to change the subject, he asked hesitantly: 'Please tell me if I intrude, sir, but do I take it that you never wished to marry?'

Parkin shook his head, chuckling. 'Marry? Dear me, no! There *was* a young lady that I was fond of once, but she married into a, shall we say, *larger* banking family. To tell the truth I would have liked to have had children of my own. There is my niece Cassandra of course, but I envy your father having sons such as you venturing forth. It would be grand to share those adventures vicariously, as it were. But in any event, a wife would have protested at my wittering on about the Romans and would no doubt have objected to the dissection of creatures on the dining room table!'

So *that* explained the old gentleman's reference to rats – and the anatomical drawings and stuffed animals in glass cases. Anson laughed. 'And she would have had a point! I have no objection to hearing about the Romans myself – on the contrary. And some fellows cook and eat rats at sea in preference to salt beef—'

Parkin's eyebrows soared. 'Good gracious!'

'Indeed, although I have never felt inclined to join them myself. And as to dissecting such creatures on the dining table, well, I can think of more agreeable pastimes!'

'Ah, but to me the pursuit of knowledge is akin to some men's obsession with the hunt. There is much satisfaction to be had from discovering what a rat had for his dinner or how a bat's wing is constructed – and recording the information I discover with my drawings. And another plus is that my second cousins steer well clear of me and my dissected rats and bats, although fortunately Cassandra has been, shall we say, brought up with them.'

It was Anson's turn to raise his eyebrows in mock alarm and, as they walked, he endeavoured to steer their discussions towards his host's passion for antiquities, rather than creatures' innards, as well as quizzing him for the latest news of the mutiny.

Parkin regaled his guest with tales of the Roman occupation, of the coming of the Jutes to East Kent and Viking raids on the Isle of Sheppey, commenting: 'If you've been there you may well have met some of their descendants!'

In return, Anson recalled some of his adventures since joining the navy as a fresh-faced midshipman, encounters with the enemy and the taking of prizes.

As a former banker, Parkin was fascinated to hear how prize money was shared, exclaiming: 'Better than gilts!'

'Yes, for officers who get the major share, but you could easily lose a body part in the winning of it – or on some other risky enterprise. Lord Nelson is a prime example.'

When pressed, Anson recounted the happenings of the past few weeks – his mission to Portsmouth carrying documents that confirmed the ending of the Spithead mutiny, and his less successful assignment to the Nore where he was greeted with a sea of red flags.

The old man was as spellbound about these adventures as Anson was about his host's antiquarian and natural history tales. Despite the wide difference in their ages the two got along famously and, with such convivial company, good food and plenty of rest, Anson's health improved rapidly.

The colour was back in his once-sallow cheeks, the lump on his head acquired through his fall had disappeared, and he was putting back the weight he had lost over the past fortnight.

\*\*\*\*

The pair were in the summerhouse reading the London newspapers and discussing the latest news of the mutiny when a letter arrived for Anson.

Immediately he knew it must be from Captain Wills at Chatham. No-one else knew where he was.

Parkin watched expectantly as Anson broke the seal, read it quickly and told his host: 'This is what I have been expecting – a summons back to Chatham. I am told they have a special service for me, and it can only be something to do with the mutiny. I must leave at first light tomorrow.'

The old man nodded. 'Very well. I'll tell the maids to pack your dunnage. Everything is clean and neatly pressed, by-the-by, and I'll arrange for my coachman to take you back in my carriage. In fact, unless you have any objection, I'll accompany you myself. It will be an outing for me.'

Anson was supervising the packing of his bag by the two giggling maids when he heard a crunch of wheels in the driveway and looked out of the window to see Josiah Parkin handing a young lady down from a carriage.

His niece, no doubt.

He descended the broad staircase in time to see Parkin enter the hallway with the pretty dark-haired young lady on his arm.

'Ah! Anson, allow me to present my niece, Cassandra.'

He bowed. 'Pleased to meet you, Miss ...?'

She bobbed and smiled, revealing perfect teeth. 'Parkin. I'm Miss *Parkin*, my uncle's brother's daughter, but as much like his own daughter as it's possible to be.'

Anson was still working that out when Parkin explained, beaming affectionately at her: 'Cassandra was the only daughter of my brother

Jeremiah and his wife Helen. Sadly we lost them to typhoid when she was a baby and she has lived with me ever since.'

'So by now you must be as well acquainted with rats as we sailors are, Miss, *er*, Parkin?'

She laughed prettily. 'I see you have learned of my uncle's foibles, sir. Fortunately his rats, squirrels, rabbits and other creatures arrive not on foot or out of holes in the skirting board, but hanging from gamekeepers' belts all ready for dissection. But in any event my uncle has encouraged me to take an interest in natural history, although I prefer flora to fauna.'

Parkin smiled benignly at his niece. 'My dear, Mister Anson is a naval officer, a lieutenant no less, resting here for a while convalescing from a fever before returning to duty at Chatham.'

'I am sorry to hear of your indisposition, Lieutenant Anson, and trust you are on the road to recovery.'

'Pretty well, Miss, *er*, Parkin, pretty well. So, from your Christian name, am I to take it that you have the gift of foresight?'

'Cassandra? I see that you know your mythology, sir. But are you aware that the Greek Kassandra, with a K rather than a C, was also known as "she who entangles men"?'

Anson exchanged a knowing glance with Parkin. 'I see that you have educated your niece well, sir. I was aware of Cassandra's gift of seeing into the future, but not about entangling men!'

'It's a little early for that sort of entanglement. My niece is only just turned sixteen, after all. But yes, I have done my best to further her education and she knows her mythology, history, literature and so on pretty well.'

'Then she is a credit to you, sir.'

Parkin shook his head. 'I fear I have cruelly neglected the more ladylike pursuits – embroidery, painting, music, dancing and suchlike.'

She laughed. 'Nonsense, uncle! Those are mere pastimes for silly girls destined to become submissive decorative wives of wealthy men. I would sooner exercise my mind rather than my needle!'

Anson thought immediately of his own two sisters who spent their lives at just such pastimes – gossiping, and sizing up all well-off eligible males within striking distance as possible husbands. Cassandra Parkin was clearly a different kettle of fish altogether.

\*\*\*\*

Dinner that evening at Ludden Hall was one of the most pleasant occasions Anson had enjoyed for many a month.

The affection between uncle and niece was infectious and the conversation ranged far and wide, from the habits of potter bees and other curiosities of natural history to be explored in the grounds to the straightness of Roman roads and the survival of Anglo-Saxon place-names.

When Parkin steered their chatter to life in the navy, Cassandra was fascinated to discover that Anson had joined as a thirteen-year-old, exclaiming: 'Goodness, I was still playing with my dolls at that age!'

She laughed charmingly at his tales of being tricked by older members of the midshipmen's berth into searching for the golden rivet, being sent to hear the dogfish bark or to ask the purser for a hammock ladder, and being mast-headed for not knowing his foremost edge from his bitter end. 'A part of a sail and a rope's end,' he explained.

'Can you recall, Lieutenant Anson, at what stage did you cease being the butt of your fellow midshipmen's jokes?'

'Oh, as soon as someone younger than I came on board,' he admitted.

'At which point you became one of the tormenters rather than the tormented?'

Anson laughed. 'Very perceptive, Miss Parkin. That *is* the natural order of things, but no, I never saw the need to subject the youngsters to such torture. Life at sea is hard enough for them as it is.'

'When did you, as it were, come of age and become a lieutenant?'

'Ah, thereby hangs a tale. It's necessary to have six years' sea service after which there is an examination—'

'Just like school?'

'I can assure you that it's a far greater ordeal than any test at school. Worse than the labours of Hercules! I had to attend a board with my certificates and logs and was subjected to an interrogation from a trio of extremely grumpy old captains who insisted that I convince them of my diligence and sobriety and asked me the most impossible questions about such things as seamanship, gunnery and, worst of all, navigation, which was never my strongest subject. I was reduced to a quivering, stuttering imbecile.'

'But you passed?'

'Yes, to everyone's astonishment, not least my own, they passed me, and then it was just a matter of waiting for a commission to a ship when a vacancy for a lieutenant occurred. It helps speed things up if you have what's euphemistically known in the service as "interest" – the support of senior people, but I have none.'

Parkin was puzzled. 'Yet your surname indicates a kinship with the great Admiral George Anson, does it not?'

It was what he was *always* asked and he shook his head slowly and confessed: 'Only a very distant kinsman, I fear, many times removed ...'

Nevertheless he was finding the evening's conversation in such amiable company most entertaining and enjoyable.

And although normally reticent about the rigours of life afloat when talking to ladies, Anson found himself cheerfully answering questions from Cassandra and her uncle on everything from flag signals to flogging.

Cassandra was especially intrigued about the crowded living conditions at sea but supposed the wardrooms for officers must be palatial compared to the sardine-like crowding of the sailors.

Anson laughed at the thought. 'I fear I have yet to come across a wardroom anything *like* a palace in a ship of the line – and of course our frigates do not even run to a wardroom. Their officers inhabit the gunroom instead. But in the navy we grow used to living cheek by jowl and any rough edges one may start out with are very soon smoothed out!'

While they were eating the conversation turned to food at sea and she again laughed charmingly on hearing that kippers were "Spithead pheasants" and tapioca pudding was known as "fishes' eyes" in the navy. Out of delicacy Anson chose not to mention "babies' heads" – the sailors' slang for steak and kidney puddings.

He also thought it wise not to stray to the consumption of rats by impoverished and half-starved midshipmen. She might be happy to observe her uncle dissecting them but, like him, would most likely draw the line at eating one, he surmised.

The two men lingered talking for a while after she had left them to their port, and it was with some reluctance that he finally dragged himself away to get what sleep he could before the morrow's journey.

# 9 - A Neutral Officer

Alone together in the coach next morning, Parkin cautiously enquired about Anson's prospects.

'I hope to make post – captain, that is. But after that, well, a naval career is something of a lottery dependent on a great many variables: whether or not you have influential friends on high – the "interest" that I mentioned; and luck, of course. Luck is everything. Some can go through their service without seeing any significant action, yet others—'

'And, as you pointed out, Nelson is a case in point?'

'Indeed, life at sea for him has been full of incident and his career is no doubt far from over yet. He is capable of more great deeds.'

The old man asked: 'I am intrigued to know what you will do *after* the navy?'

Anson laughed. 'Is there such a thing?'

Parkin appeared not to notice the irony and asked: 'I believe you mentioned that you were the Reverend Anson's second son?'

'That's correct, sir. My brother Gussie will inherit, such as it is. The local squire has the advowson—'

'The power to appoint the rector?'

'Yes, my father owes his living and therefore his allegiance to the Brax family rather than the church itself. But why do you ask—?'

Parkin put up his hands. 'Merely my inquisitive nature, but no matter – let's talk of happier things.'

'Rats?' Anson asked mischievously.

'Why not rats, indeed, both ashore and afloat? And of the eternal search for the golden rivet!'

\*\*\*\*

At Chatham, Anson asked to be put down at the main gate and as they made their farewells he asked his host: 'How can I begin to thank you, sir? You have truly been a Good Samaritan.'

'Nonsense, my boy. My niece and I have much enjoyed your company and if the opportunity arises I trust you will call upon us again, in a less dramatic fashion, I hope. We country mice are starved of agreeable company.'

Anson raised his hat. 'I will indeed, sir. Please give Miss, *er*, Cassandra my compliments. I will write to you once I have joined my ship in the Mediterranean to record my thanks – and give account of what occurs after we part.'

The old man was clearly touched. 'That would give me a great deal of pleasure.' And, waving farewell, he rapped his gold-topped cane on the carriage door and ordered his coachman: 'Walk on!'

\*\*\*\*

The gatehouse guards showed little interest in Anson. To them he was just another officer among the many, and, rather than keeping visitors out, their chief duty was preventing dockyard workers making off with official stores.

The guards directed Anson to the commissioner's house where on arrival he was ushered immediately into the presence of Captain Wills.

'Ah, Anson, isn't it?' Waving him to a chair, the captain enquired: 'So you've not been well, but you've had a good long rest, I hope?'

It would take too long to explain in any detail, so Anson responded: 'Indeed, sir, and I am back to full strength and ready to be of service.' He well knew he was stretching the truth in claiming to be fully fit, but this was not a time for sounding feeble.

'Good, good! Well, we have a role for you. I recall that you told Admiral Buckner you were willing to undertake any mission that might arise while waiting for the store-ship to take passage for the Med?'

'Indeed, sir.'

'Well, such a mission has arisen. May I take it that you have kept yourself up to speed with the so-called mutiny?'

'I have, sir, insofar as one can glean a true picture from the news-sheets.'

The captain grimaced. 'Hmm, in my book there never was an inky-fingered gutter press scribbler who got the facts straight, but I suppose we can't entirely blame them if we in the navy keep things close to our chests, eh? And it wouldn't do for them to print the truth about our dispositions and whatnot and give the French valuable intelligence, would it now?'

Anson smiled agreement. He had long since learned that most senior officers abhorred openness and favoured maintaining a silent service, no doubt for good reasons. He had heard that smugglers based in the

Channel ports regularly took the latest newspapers across to France – for a price.

Wills leaned forward conspiratorially. 'Well, the latest situation is that the hotheads among the so-called delegates, led by that reprobate Parker, have been trying to persuade the rest to blockade London itself, or even to desert to the French, for God's sake! They've been flogging any of their shipmates who've refused to join them, and now we hear they're planning to take the ships to sea, although I doubt there's enough support for that.'

'I had heard of the blockade proposal, and that some are for deserting to the enemy. Either course would be a very serious escalation, would it not, sir?'

'Just so, and many of the men know it. We have reliable information that a good number wish to *un*-mutiny or whatever the opposite to mutiny is. If they were sheep, which you could argue they are, it would be a case of returning to the fold …'

'Indeed, sir.'

'But they are afraid of what the other mutineers might do to them if they back out, and at the same time they are nervous of the reception they'll get from us if they bring their ships in. Would we flog 'em or string 'em up from their own yardarms …?'

He pondered for a moment as if imagining such a fate. 'Only natural to worry about such things if you've been in a mutiny I suppose?'

Anson nodded. 'Quite understandable, sir.'

'Put simply, they are damned if they do, and damned if they don't. But some sensible men have bitten the bullet and offered to break free and turn themselves and their ship in. You know *Euphemus*?'

'Only as one of our sixty-fours, sir.'

'Well, now they've had a chance to stew in their own juice, sniffed the noose, seen the error of their ways and so forth, many of *Euphemus's* people want to throw in the towel. They have sent a boat here to seek confirmation that the dockyard is not controlled by mutineers and that the ship will be received safely and not fired upon by shore batteries if she effects an escape. They are particularly nervous of the Sheerness batteries and all the yeomanry bumpkins milling around there, so have opted to come here.'

'So, sir, what part do you wish me to play? Is it to help bring her in here, to Chatham?'

'No, that could prove too tricky. Sheerness is far closer and I've given the men who've come here the admiral's personal assurance that *Euphemus* will be welcomed back there with open arms.'

'So …?'

Wills smiled. 'So, among the requests these *un*-mutineers have put is for an officer to be sent to help do just that '

Anson was puzzled. 'But if they sent their officers ashore when the red flags were raised, the captain etcetera will be available to take command again?'

'Ah, sadly that cannot be. The problem is that the men had become, shall we say, *disenchanted* with their officers. There are still some hotheads on board *Euphemus* and if one of their own officers returns, the whole mutiny thing could kick off again. No, what's needed now is a neutral officer, someone not tainted by what's occurred. In short, you …'

Elbows on the desk, he clasped his hands together and fixed Anson with a not unfriendly stare. 'You must be aware that this temporary command could well turn out to be a poisoned chalice. I cannot be certain that the rest of the ship's company will welcome you on board, and even if you are able to break free from the other ships there is every possibility that some or all will open fire on you.'

Anson shrugged. 'Nevertheless, sir, I am happy to accept.'

Wills smiled, obviously relieved that he had a willing volunteer. 'Handsome of you, Anson! In all honesty I cannot exactly wish you joy of such a brief and tainted first command, but I can assure you that if you can pull this off it will not be forgotten. By-the-by, how's your mythology?'

'Sir?

'Are you aware of the origin of *Euphemus*?'

Anson pondered, trying to recall the Greek mythology learned from his classics-obsessed father. 'Wasn't he the helmsman for Jason and the Argonauts in their quest for the golden fleece?'

Wills nodded. 'Correct! He was a son of Poseidon and Europa and had the gift of moving over the sea so swiftly that his feet remained dry.'

'I hope I manage to keep mine dry too, sir, but I daresay that'll be tricky in a tidal river with mudflats and all. I have to confess I'm not the navy's most able navigator or seaman, not by a long chalk—'

'This is not about navigation or seamanship, Anson. What's required in these circumstances is leadership.'

'But do I take it that the sailing master is still on board and that I can talk to the boat's crew before we leave?'

'The sailing master is indeed on board, although I hear he's a bit of an old woman, inclined to be overly cautious.'

'That might not come amiss, sir.'

The captain smiled. 'You could be right. Anyway, let's get to it. The boat's crew are waiting nearby to meet you. I confess I have built up your reputation somewhat, near kin of the great Admiral Lord Anson and all that, but I'm confident you will measure up to it!'

****

Captain Wills led the way to a private office where seven men were sitting round a table, evidently in earnest discussion. They made to rise as he entered but he waved them to sit.

'This, men, is the Lieutenant Anson I was telling you about. He is a fine officer, a member of the great Admiral Anson's family, and has been travelling while all this mutiny business has been going on, so he is, shall we say, untainted ...'

The men nodded and their leader said: 'We're obliged, sir.'

Wills added: 'The bosun, here, Mister Rook, has been appointed—'

Rook interrupted: '*Elected*, sir.'

The captain looked doubtful. Elections were not normally known in the navy and like all officers he was deeply suspicious of lower deck politicking. But he shrugged. 'Very well, *elected* by the loyal men to lead them back to the paths of righteousness. I refer, of course, to their ship's escape from the mutinous fleet.'

Rook rose. 'It's true that I've been elected, sir, but I'd like to make it plain that I'm not what they're calling "a delegate". All the ships chose delegates to put their grievances forward when the mutiny kicked off, but I didn't want to be one of them.' This was understandable for a warrant officer of his standing.

'Are the *Euphemus* delegates on board now?' the captain asked.

'No, sir. They are away at some meeting with Parker planning to blockade London, but the rest of us … well, *most* of us … want to jack it in and bring her in. *That's* what I've been elected to do.'

Anson sized the boatswain up and liked what he saw. Rook was a broad-shouldered man of a type he had come across many a time in his naval career: tough, alert, and – he believed – dependable. It was easy to understand why his shipmates had chosen him to lead them in the absence of their officers and the so-called delegates with whom they had become disenchanted.

Captain Wills continued: 'Lieutenant Anson has offered to return to *Euphemus* with you and help you take her in to Sheerness, so are you still up for it?'

Rook looked around at his nodding shipmates before speaking for them. 'We are, sir.'

'Good men! But understand this, who elected whom and for why is of no interest whatsoever to me. If this is to work you must accept Lieutenant Anson here as your leader, your temporary captain. A lot could go wrong in this venture and you and the loyal men back on board must accept his orders without question. Is that perfectly clear?'

They exchanged glances again and Rook spoke for all. 'Aye, sir, perfectly clear.'

'Good. Now, I'll say it again in front of this officer, just so's we're all singing from the same hymnbook. You have my personal assurance on behalf of the admiral himself that you won't be fired on when you bring your ship in and that every man jack aboard will be given a pardon covering anything any of them might have done during the mutiny. Like at Spithead, it'll apply to all who return to duty. One of the clerks is busy putting that on paper at this very moment and I'll sign it for you to take with you just in case you need to convince any doubting shipmates.'

They nodded their appreciation.

'Good, then I'll leave you to make your plans with Lieutenant Anson. But before I go let me say that much depends upon you. If you can bring *Euphemus* in safely I truly believe the mutiny will crumble and the navy will be able to get back to its rightful business of fighting the French. It's not over-stating the case to say that the fate of our country lies in your hands.'

They rose as he made to leave, and at the door he turned as if struck by an after-thought. He delved into his pocket for a small leather-bound book. 'Anson, men, I almost forgot that I meant to remind you of Francis Drake's prayer. You are all familiar with it, are you not?'

Puzzled looks revealed that they were not, but Wills appeared not to notice. 'It is most apt for men in your shoes ...'

He opened the book, cleared his throat and read:

*"O Lord God, when Thou givest to Thy servants to endeavour any great matter, grant us also to know that it is not the beginning but the continuing of the same until it be thoroughly finished which yieldeth the true glory."*

Captain Wills looked around the table and repeated slowly: 'Continuing until it be *thoroughly* finished ... Is that clear?'

Then to muttered agreement he snapped the book shut and left without further ado.

Anson took a seat and looked at each man in turn. Their faces were anxious but they appeared to be the sort of men you could rely on and he broke the silence and provoked nervous smiles with: 'Now, I reckon God's got his hands pretty full so I try not to bother him too much myself, gentlemen, but I have to admit that having singed the King of Spain's beard at Cadiz and helped see off the Spanish Armada, Drake's words were worth hearing.'

Pausing for effect and a subdued chuckle, Anson told the men: 'I suggest you introduce yourselves and then we'll work out how we're going to steal your ship back for the King!'

# 10 - Strike the Red Flag

With Rook at the tiller and Anson crouching in the thwarts, a long-barrelled sea service pistol in his belt, the boat was rowed back down the Medway.

It was a long haul for the oarsmen but at last they rounded the Isle of Grain, opposite Sheerness, and emerged into the Great Nore anchorage.

Now, with oars muffled, the boat was rowed as silently as possible through ships of the line, frigates and store-ships, all seen merely as shadowy outlines on this pitch-black night.

From one they could hear the scrape of a fiddle, singing and snatches of raucous laughter. But others lay totally silent like great wallowing leviathans. And as they slipped past one, someone threw a bucketful of gash over the side, narrowly missing the boat.

Thank the Lord the boat's crew knew where they were going, Anson thought, when at last they shipped oars and graunched alongside a three-decker, HMS *Euphemus* he guessed.

Ignoring the normal rule of senior officer last in, first out, it was Rook who signalled Anson to stay put, gripped the netting hanging from the ship's side, and disappeared up into the darkness.

Anson presumed, correctly, that he had gone to report the success of their mission and to warn the ship's company that the neutral officer they had requested was about to board.

There was a low whistle from above and one of the oarsmen nudged Anson and pointed upwards. He rose, gripped the netting and hauled himself up.

After what he had been through over past weeks it was a great effort to claw his way up and he arrived on deck gasping for breath and feeling weak.

A small knot of men awaited him and Rook introduced him, curtly. 'This is Lieutenant Anson. He's not been involved in all of this and we have the admiral's word that he's all right and wants to help us.'

There was a murmur of acceptance and the bosun muttered: 'Let's go below, boys, and sort out what needs to be done.'

But as they passed others on their way below Anson noted that there were some with sullen, suspicious looks. Clearly the desire to end the mutiny was not universal.

In the captain's cabin Anson was introduced to the sailing master, William Sadler, and the sergeant of marines, the stocky Devonian Josh Kennard. Both, he knew, would be key to the business in hand.

The bosun's mates and Kennard and his marines could, he hoped, be relied upon to keep order and confine any malcontents who showed signs of giving trouble.

And having the master on board was a godsend. Navigation was Sadler's province and hopefully he knew his way around the estuary mudflats, which Anson certainly did not.

The senior warrant officer on board, the master was appointed, like the bosun, by the Navy Board rather than the Admiralty. Anson was familiar with his role – setting courses, finding the ship's position, supervising the pilotage – and that most important duty to "represent to the captain every possible danger in or near to the ship's course, and the way to avoid it."

As temporary, unpaid, acting captain, Anson sincerely hoped the latter would apply this night.

But, shaking the man's hand, he confined himself to saying: 'You and I will likely have a busy night, master.'

Sadler nodded nervously. 'Can't say as it's going to be easy, sir. Everything's agin us.'

Anson immediately sensed the man's lack of confidence was going to be a problem and hoped it wasn't catching.

Gratefully accepting a chair, Anson declined the offer of a drink, and, looking around the enlarged group, told them: 'Let's be clear, gentlemen …' his use of the word was deliberate, '… if I am to take command and help you take the ship in there must be *no* drinking. It'll be tricky enough stone cold sober. I'd be obliged, Mister Rook, if you'd kindly place reliable guards on all sources of liquor.'

The bosun signalled across the table and Sergeant Kennard sent his corporal to make it so.

Anson paused to let the drink ban sink in and detected no opposition.

'Now,' he said, 'let's also be clear that I understand the requests that have been made by the delegates and the reasons for them, and, I can tell you, I am not unsympathetic.'

There were murmurs of approval and he decided to level with them. 'Look, I was in Portsmouth a while back and let me tell you if you didn't already know, that the Spithead men got pretty well all they asked for. I know because I carried the Admiralty's response down there.'

Puzzled looks were exchanged around the table and the men's leader held up his hand.

'Yes, Mister Rook?'

'We were told you *weren't* involved. You were like, neutral. But now you tell us—'

Anson checked him. 'Look, I happened to call at the Admiralty to sort out my next ship. They needed a messenger boy and I was lurked for the job. Until I got to Portsmouth I'd no idea what I was carrying.'

He sensed this was a critical moment. If they lost confidence in him now, all would be hazarded.

Looking around at the doubting faces, he raised both hands to halt the muttering. 'The problem here, gentlemen, is not that I was a reluctant messenger, but that just when the pardon and most concessions were being granted to the Spithead men, the Nore so-called delegates chose not to believe assurances that the same applied to *all* of you ...'

'We know that,' Rook accepted.

'But now that they've decided to try and blockade London and some are even advocating sailing to join the French, well, like most of you, I think that's more than a step too far to put it mildly. They're playing into the hands of the enemy and putting the whole country in peril.'

'That's right, sir,' the bosun agreed. 'We ain't at war with England, are we boys?'

The rest assented and Anson knew the crisis had passed.

He told them: 'Like you, I serve King and country. I have no truck with disobedience and mutiny, and seeing as how you sent to ask for help to bring the ship in, I believe that most if not all of you share my view. Is that so?'

Heads were nodded and there was a consensus of agreement around the table.

Anson breathed a sigh of relief. 'Very well, then let's get to the task in hand. Master, we'll need to take her in under cover of darkness, otherwise the rest of the fleet might fire upon us when they smoke what we're at ...'

Sadler nodded. 'That's right, sir. But, like I said, it won't be easy. There's lots of mudflats. All the channel markers have been sunk by Trinity House and they've moved the Nore buoy and lightship. We'll be going in blind ...'

Anson only just managed to stop himself exclaiming 'Good grief!' It was news to him that all the navigational aids had gone, but he readily understood why. The Trinity House men were responsible for the provision and maintenance of these aids and had no doubt been prevailed upon to make life as difficult as possible for the mutineers. Without the markers and buoys it would be difficult, dangerous even, for the mutinous ships anchored near the mudflats to manoeuvre, and many were effectively trapped.

He could see that the pilot's warning had cast doubt among the others and realised it was a time to be forceful. 'Mister Sadler, I am aware of the degree of difficulty, but our task is to take her into Sheerness. You are right to voice these warnings. It's your duty to do so. But attempt it we must, and you are key to that.'

'But if we go tonight the tide will be against us, sir.'

'Tide, or no tide, we'll take her in anyway.'

Sadler looked boot-faced, but there was nothing for it. The ship's company were for breaking free and if he was able to pull it off he would be safe from the noose himself. But he could not stop himself from muttering: 'It'll be more than my repitation's worth if we end up stranded on a mudflat ...'

Anson ignored the whinge. 'Right, gentlemen, let's get to it, but I'd like Mister Sadler, the bosun, and you, sergeant, to hang back for a moment to go through a few points.'

The rest got to their feet and left talking animatedly among themselves.

Once alone with the select group, Anson told them: 'Gentlemen, this is the situation. We are going in whatever it takes. Sergeant Kennard, kindly make sure that those of your men who can be trusted are armed, and I would like you to stick close to me.'

The sergeant looked daggers.

'What's wrong, sergeant?'

'*All* the marines can be trusted, sir, even the micks.'

Anson smiled and said with exaggerated gravity. 'Of course! I meant no disrespect, and certainly not to our Irish marines! In uncertain times like this one forgets to give credit to those upon whom we can *always* rely.'

Somewhat mollified, the sergeant excused himself to gather his men.

Anson turned to Rook. 'You tell me there are many others among the ship's company you can truly depend upon, so kindly send them on deck. I want no piped orders and you must pass the word for every man to go about his duties quietly. If we attract the attention of the other ships we'll be dead in the water.'

'Aye, aye, sir!'

The bosun clattered away but Anson held Sadler back. 'Now, master, let's take a look at the chart and check our position and our best course. I confess to being thoroughly disorientated after being rowed here in the dark.'

Sadler produced a chart and they pored over it by the great cabin's flickering lantern light.

Anson took a coin from his purse. 'Kindly mark our position and take me through the best course for the dockyard.'

Sadler looked doubtful.

'You are not, I hope, about to tell me that you don't *know* our position.'

'Not for certain, sir. You see, like I said, the Trinity House people have got rid of all the navigational markers, deliberate-like, to confuse the mutineers.'

'Good grief! So we don't know where we are, nor where we're going?'

'Not rightly, sir, no. Of course, I know *roughly* where we are …'

He hesitatingly placed the coin on the chart and then moved it inch or two, adding, in a somewhat exasperated tone: 'The trouble is we've been swinging around at anchor for a couple of weeks or more and the mudflats hereabouts are, well, changeable-like. Very confusing at the best of times—'

'And these are not the best of times?'

'You could say that, sir. Like I warned at the meeting, everything's agin us, tide and all.'

'Nevertheless, we have no choice but to make a run for it, so let's get to it. We'll weigh anchor and get under way before dawn else we surely risk being fired upon by ships still loyal to the delegates.'

\*\*\*\*

On deck, preparations were being made in almost complete silence lest nearby ships caught on to what was happening.

Anson watched in the thin pre-dawn light until the sailing master reported to him that all was ready. 'Very well, Mister Sadler, set fore-topsail.'

The master turned to the bosun and repeated huskily: 'Set fore-topsail.'

Rook passed the order to waiting foretop-men who began clambering silently up the rigging.

But from high above came a shout: 'On deck there! I'll blow the brains out of any man that so much as touches a sail!'

Anson cursed inwardly. So much for keeping silence …

Every eye went up to where a figure was spotted on the top yard, brandishing a pistol.

Rook muttered savagely: 'Who the devil's that and where did he get that pistol?'

The man shouted: 'On deck there! Take no notice of this bleedin' orficer, mates. He's been sent to make us betray our brothers. If you take the ship in you might as well put nooses round your own necks. Long live the mutiny!'

There were some cries of support from men who had been hanging back, but most of those on deck shouted them down. The bosun muttered: 'It's that bloody fool Clegg. He must have got at the armoury while we were ashore. And the spirit locker, likely as not. The daft bastard'll alert every ship in the fleet!'

He cupped his hands and shouted: 'Come down Clegg! The mutiny's a dead duck and we're taking the ship in, whether you like it or not. Get yourself down here. Now!'

'Come and get me if you like, but I'll take you to hell with me!'

Sergeant Kennard stepped forward with a primed musket and aimed it at the man, shouting: 'I'll count to ten!'

He began to count and there was stalemate until he reached nine. But then there was a ragged cheer from the loyal hands on deck as Clegg lowered his pistol and the waiting foretop-men recommenced climbing the rigging.

The marine sergeant was taking no chances and called up to the man to throw his pistol down. After a moment's hesitation he did so, but as it hit the deck it went off with a loud crack. The ball flew harmlessly out to sea, but everyone on deck froze. The shouting may well have alerted other ships, but the shot was *certain* to have been heard, drawing unwelcome attention to *Euphemus* just as they were about to get under way.

Silence was pointless now and Anson told the bosun: 'Order them to look lively now. We are living on borrowed time.'

But the bosun's shouted encouragement was unnecessary. Aloft, gaskets were cast off and the sail billowed down on the restraining clew lines, buntlines and slab lines.

In turn these were let go, and on deck below men at the sheets and braces trimmed the canvas. All eyes were on the foretop-sail which flapped and then drew.

Anson turned to the master. 'Weigh, Mister Sadler.'

'Weigh it is, sir!' And, without needing orders, the waiting men, led by the marines, swarmed to the capstan and took up their positions half a dozen to each of the twelve bars, with two more on each swifter – the ropes that linked the bars.

This procedure, Anson knew only too well, was going to take time. The cable was too thick to be turned round the capstan, so its lower spindle on the gun-deck below was used to receive a messenger rope. As the anchor cable came through the hawse hole, temporary lashings – nippers – were used to attach it to the messenger which was then wound in via the capstan.

As the anchor rose, the lashings had to be reattached near the hawse hole and the recovered cable fed down a hatchway to the orlop deck for storage, and there were more than enough willing hands to do the manhandling.

Another group was already positioned on the forecastle, ready to hook the anchor ring with the cat tackle when it broke surface and secure it to the cathead.

And the nippers – the youngest hands whose job was to nip the anchor cable to the endless belt activated by the capstan – were standing ready.

But Anson was far from confident. However well-schooled the men were this was a tricky operation at the best of times and could easily become chaotic if they came under heavy fire and the urge to take cover became irresistible.

He looked up and saw that the first streaks of dawn were now clearly illuminating the red flag still flying at the main masthead.

'Bosun!'

'Sir?'

'Strike the red flag and hoist the royal standard. We'll take her in wearing the King's colour, no less!'

# 11 - Under Fire

But as the red flag came fluttering down and the royal standard was run up to mark their departure from the mutinous fleet, it was clear from distant shouts that the move had been spotted from at least one of the nearby ships.

A gun barked and the ball splashed a few yards ahead of *Euphemus*. It was followed seconds later by another from a different ship, and then a third opened fire. These were warning shots but it was clear that they were in imminent danger of coming under sustained fire.

The master looked to Anson and cried out in alarm. 'If we delay weighing anchor we're dead ducks!' And, stating the blindingly obvious, he croaked: 'It's dawning and they have our range, sir.'

Anson deliberated for a few seconds. It was true that raising the anchor would take time – time they did not have.

Dawn was indeed breaking, but abandoning a valuable anchor went against the grain. However, there was always a possibility that it could be recovered from these shallow waters.

'Very well, Mister Sadler, I hear you. Bosun, cut away the anchor, but mark its position with a buoy.'

'Aye, aye, sir! There's a buoy already attached.'

Rook sent a seaman to fetch axes, snatched one and began chopping away at the thick rope cable. Two others joined him, swinging their axes in turn.

After a dozen blows it parted and the severed end splashed down into the muddy water, temporarily dragging the buoy under with it. Immediately the filled fore-topsail impelled the ship forward with a shuddering lurch to the cheers of the loyal crewmen on deck.

Anson watched as the buoy bobbed to the surface marking the anchor's resting place and braced himself against the ship's forward movement.

The break for freedom was under way at last. Now that their intention was clear the time for warning shots was over and he steeled himself for the real thing.

But for whatever reason, the other ships ceased firing as *Euphemus* surged forward on a strengthening easterly breeze.

He called for a glass and, leaning against the mainmast for support, raised it to his eye with both hands and swept the nearest ships. Some sort of altercation was going on aboard the nearest and Anson could only surmise it was because some of the gunners were loath to fire on their own shipmates.

Snapping the telescope shut he called to the master. 'What depth do we have, Mister Sadler?'

The master was monitoring the leadsman's calls. 'It's tricky, sir, varying between five and ten fathoms by the minute. It's these blessed mudflats, you see, and we can't be far away from the Middleground Shoal. It's *somewhere* hereabouts ...'

But his answer tailed off as the ship's progress came to a sudden shuddering halt and all on deck were thrown around with great violence.

Anson was helped to his feet by the bosun. He retrieved his hat and the telescope and looked across at the master who had also been thrown off his feet and was struggling to get up. 'I presume, Mister Sadler, that we have just discovered your Middleground Shoal?'

'Aye, sir,' the master answered ruefully, 'I'm very much afraid that we have, and now we really *are* sitting ducks. You will recall, sir, I did warn that this could very well happen.'

Anson reacted irritably. 'Yes, yes, Mister Sadler! It's exactly as you warned, and unless we do something about it, and quickly at that, we'll sit here helpless before the delegates' guns. But kindly refrain from reminding me what I already know and advise me on what we can *do* about it.' He was not normally one to chide others in front of their underlings, but he could no longer hide his irritation.

Sadler flushed, but before he could answer, first one then another of the ships still under the delegates' control recommenced firing on *Euphemus*, directly this time. These were no longer warning shots but were aimed high, doubtless to damage cordage and canvas to ensure that the escaping ship went nowhere.

The gunners, Anson acknowledged, had adopted the French style of attempting to cut away sails and rigging, leaving the hull undamaged. Even the most radical were no doubt reluctant to kill fellow-seamen, some of whom were no doubt still sympathetic to the mutiny, unnecessarily.

He called the bosun, Hogg, the acting gunner, Connor, the carpenter, and the pilot to a quick council of war.

'Well, Mister Sadler, what can we do? Lying here we're as helpless as a stranded whale and at the mercy of the delegates' guns.'

Sadler looked nervously at the others. 'I did warn you, sir ...'

Anson's patience was wearing paper-thin as the brisk gunfire continued and more of the rigging fell about them.

'No-one's blaming you, master. The responsibility is *mine*. But if you have nothing more constructive to say I suggest—'

But before he could finish the bosun chipped in: 'We'll need to get her off this shoal, sir, and in short order or else the waverers will turn again and vote to re-join the mutiny. And if they do that I wouldn't give a lot for our chances – or yours.'

The handful of men around him waited expectantly and Anson knew that only drastic and immediate action would give them a chance of getting out of their predicament.

'Very well,' he said, with all the calmness he could muster, 'this is what we must do. We'll run her lower deck guns over the side to lighten her, and then try kedging her off.'

The master nodded. 'All things considered in these dire circumstances, that's about the best we could do, sir.'

A mite sarcastically, Anson answered: 'Thank you for expressing your confidence in my plan so eloquently, Mister Sadler. Now, bosun, see to it that the guns are ditched and lower the kedge anchor into the boat we came in. Pick the strongest oarsmen and tell them they are to row like hell into the navigable channel and heave it in. Once that's done, call for volunteers to man the capstan bars again and we'll heave ourselves off. Go to it. Time is of the essence!'

The bosun knuckled his forehead. 'Aye, aye, sir.'

Hogg had registered horror at the thought of some of his precious guns going overboard, but realised there was no alternative and wisely held his peace. Connor was already on his way to the lower gun deck, calling to his mates to bring sledgehammers and saws.

Anson called: 'Master!'

'Sir?'

'Reef sails while we have some left. If the delegates' gun crews see them come down they may think we're about to give up and will stop using our canvas for target practice.'

'Aye, aye, sir!'

Anson leant back against the mainmast, listening as his orders were relayed, and recalling incredulously that only the night before last he had been enjoying a most convivial evening with Josiah Parkin and his niece in the peaceful atmosphere of Ludden Hall. How much had happened since then ...

Loud hammering from below told him that gun ports were being knocked out, and then came cries of men heaving and a series of splashes as the guns went overboard.

Absurdly, given the circumstances, ditching the guns disturbed him even more than abandoning the anchor. But he consoled himself that when normality returned it might well be possible to recover them, given that they were on a known shoal marked on the charts.

While the rest of the guns were being manhandled overboard the kedge, the ship's smallest anchor, was lowered into the boat and oarsmen led by the bosun swarmed down the side netting to man it.

A wag shouted: 'Don't row orf wivout attaching a rope to that there anchor, bosun!'

This raised a laugh, but although Anson reckoned that Rook knew what he was doing he peered over the side to make sure the kedge anchor was indeed attached by a light cable.

The boat's crew's task was to row out into deeper water and drop the anchor which would, he hoped, stick fast in the bottom mud so that they could haul on it via the ship's capstan and literally hook themselves off.

Anson had determined to place himself alongside the heavers to underline that he had come not simply to give orders but to put himself on the line to save the ship – and all their lives.

The boat carrying the anchor was silhouetted and the mutinous gunners soon smoked what was afoot. A ball skimmed across the water from one of their ships but was fortunately well wide.

Anson debated with himself about the possibility of calling the kedging crew back, but rejected the thought. They represented his only chance of getting the ship off the mudflat and if this did not work they would remain stuck fast, wallowing helplessly at the mercy of every mutineer gunner.

Sergeant Kennard asked: 'D'you want me to get a couple of gun crews together and return fire, sir?'

Anson shook his head. 'No. If we open up on them we'll bring down the fire of every other ship on us. We'll have to take our chance and hope to haul her off.'

The master protested: 'But, sir, they're targeting the boat—'

'I don't think they were aiming at the kedging boat, Mr Sadler. It was more of a warning. There'll be those on board the mutinous ships who won't tolerate killing fellow seamen. If we recall the kedging crew we'll be doing just what they want us to do. We'll be stuck here and all they'll need do is send their own boats to re-take us. Then they can kedge us off and take us back into the bosom of the fleet. And you and I will be the first to be clapped in irons – or worse.'

Another ball scudded over the water, this time only a few yards ahead of the kedging boat.

Sadler winced and considered for a moment before agreeing. 'You're right, sir. I can see that. But the boys had better get a shift on or those gunners might just forget that they don't want to kill their comrades.'

Anson put his hand to his forehead to shield his eyes and squinted at the boat.

'Are they far enough out in the channel?'

'Another few strokes I should think, sir.'

'Bosun?'

'He's in the boat, sir!'

'Of course!' He slapped his hand to his forehead. 'Very well, master, get some of his mates to stand the men by to man the capstan.'

'Aye, aye, sir.'

Turning back to the rowers, Anson cupped his hands to his mouth and shouted: 'Ahoy the kedging crew. Are you far enough off the mud?'

The bosun's reply was faint but just audible. 'That we are, sir. Looks like we're in deep water again.'

'Then heave the anchor!'

The oarsmen shipped their oars, took hold of the kedge anchor and there was a great splash as it went over the side and sank in the channel, a stream of bubbles marking its descent until it reached bottom and one of its flukes buried itself in the thick glutinous mud.

Immediately, without the need for a further order, the rowers resumed their seats, dipped oars, manoeuvred the boat round and pulled together, a little erratically at first and then in unison back to the ship.

The dropping of the anchor had clearly been observed from the nearest mutinous ships and their guns remained silent as it was realised that they had failed to deter the kedging crew.

By the time the boat clapped on to *Euphemus's* starboard side the cable was being swiftly hauled back up and attached to the capstan.

This huge turntable on the upper deck required six men pushing each of its twelve bars that resembled the spokes of a wheel.

A large group of volunteers was being gathered by the bosun's mates – far more men than were needed. But then, Anson reckoned, it would be exhausting work and replacements would almost certainly be needed before the job was done.

The bosun and the rest of the boat's crew clambered back on deck and he and Anson pushed their way through the throng and took their places among the volunteers manning the bars.

'Ready boys?' called the bosun.

There was a chorus of 'aye, ayes' and he shouted: 'Take the strain … heave!'

The men at the bars pushed against them and at first the capstan turned freely as it took up the slack in the cable. But as the anchor bit home and the cable tautened, pushing became harder, there was virtually no movement and the men around Anson were beginning to strain, puff and blow.

Weakened by his recent illness and unused to hard physical work, he felt himself wilting.

Noting the lack of progress, other men joined their mates at the capstan bars, so that there were now seven or eight to each, heaving for all they were worth.

At last the capstan began to turn slowly and with much groaning of timbers and cheers from the hands, the ship crept forward a few inches towards the deep where the kedge anchor was holding firm.

Now that it was moving at last, Anson fell out, his lungs gasping for air, and he sank to the deck along with a number of others who, like him, had temporarily succumbed to the effort. But their places were quickly taken and the ship continued to creep forward fractionally.

All eyes were on the cable until a crack of a cannon and the splash of a ball dropping just ahead of the ship made all hands swing round in alarm. One of the mutinous ships had opened fire with what he hoped was only another warning shot.

Undeterred, the men at the capstan continued to push and Anson guessed that they were being watched closely through glasses from some of the nearby ships because almost immediately several more guns opened up on *Euphemus.*

Forcing himself back to the capstan he yelled: 'Heave, men, heave! Push like hell and let's float her off before those gunners take their fingers out and start aiming true!'

The cable, no doubt made in the new ropery at Chatham Dockyard, tautened again.

With the bosun shouting encouragement, they heaved and heaved. Seeing what needed to be done, a few more volunteers came forward and found spaces at the capstan and then slowly but surely and with much creaking *Euphemus* began to move faster, a few inches at first and then feet, then yards until at last she slumped and slithered forward off the mud-bank into the deeper water of the navigable channel.

They were free of the mud and would soon be free of the delegates' control – and free of the mutiny.

Anson, still feeling weak and exhausted from his efforts at the capstan, sat on a grating, his chest heaving.

Somehow he pulled himself together to give the orders for setting what canvas they still had to sail away to Sheerness, but there was no need. The capstan party were sprawled every which way, but other willing hands were already in the rigging setting sail and the pilot was alongside the quartermaster. They were taking the ship in.

He noted with relief that the mutinous ships had ceased firing, but why he knew not.

While his attention was elsewhere and before the ship had got fully under way a boat bumped alongside and three men clambered aboard.

Rook pushed through the exhausted capstan crew and warned Anson. 'Some delegates have come on board, sir, and they want a word with you.'

Anson raised his eyes heavenward. So that was why the firing had ceased, but this was the very last thing he needed. 'Very well, Mister Rook, bring them here.'

The newcomers were ushered to him and Anson struggled to his feet and gave them the once-over. Two, clearly seamen, were strangers to him, but he could not have been more astonished to see who the third man, clearly their leader, was.

This was a face he was very familiar with, having sat opposite the man in the mail coach from London to Portsmouth just a few short weeks before.

It was Greybeard, the man who had tried to steal the Admiralty papers from him, and it was obvious that he was no seaman.

He stared at the man. 'You! You're the one who attacked me when I got off the mail coach at Portsmouth. What in hell's name are *you* doing here?'

Greybeard sneered. 'I could ask the same of you. It's plain who you are. You're an Admiralty spy. *I'm* with the delegates.'

'Not one of them?' Anson had heard that there were revolutionary trouble-makers about, and it was rumoured that such men had been encouraged by the French to foment trouble.

Some of the ship's company who had chosen not to help heave the ship off the shoal were gathering behind the newcomers.

Greybeard addressed them. 'I've come across this jumped-up officer before, lads. He's from the Admiralty and he's been hobnobbing with the admiral down at Portsmouth. I'll bet you anything you like he's been sent here now to fool you into taking the ship in to try and break the rest of us. But I can tell you, if you continue to help him you'll be signing your death warrants. It's divide and conquer and if you give up now you'll be swinging from your own yard arm before the month's out. Throw him over the side now and we can hoist the red flag again. Your mates in the other ships will welcome you back with open arms!'

There was murmuring among the men on deck, many of them torn between continuing the escape or rejoining the mutiny.

One of the hotheads shouted. 'He's right, mates! Like as not they'll string us up if we take her into the dockyard. There's thousands of soldiers been brought in to take us on!'

Another yelled: 'Aye, that's true. There's cavalry patrolling the waterside and they've set up shore batteries. Let's rejoin the delegates afore it's too late!'

Still another joined him. 'We'll be slaughtered if we go in! Let's pack this escape nonsense in now and haul up the red flag again!'

Those both for and against began shouting. but the bosun held up his hand and shouted for silence. 'That's rubbish boys. We've been given the admiral's personal assurance that we'll be welcomed back and given a free pardon.'

Greybeard laughed sardonically. 'An admiral's personal assurance! I wouldn't give a brass farthing for one of those. Has he assured you that you'll get paid regular, allowed shore leave and all the other things we've fought for? Bet your lives he hasn't and if he has, well, sure as eggs is eggs you won't get any of it!'

The man's exhortation drew a cacophony of shouts, for and against.

It was a critical moment and Anson knew it. He stepped up on a grating so that he could be seen and waited for the shouting to die down. 'Don't listen to Greybeard here, men. I did encounter him down in Portsmouth where he was agitating to keep the Spithead mutiny going, but he's *not* your friend, and he's no seaman. He's a revolutionary, a traitor and supporter of the Frogs!'

Greybeard tried to shout him down but Anson persisted. 'As God's my witness, lads, what the bosun has told you is the truth. The admiral sent me to help you break free and I swear to you that I would not have come if you were to be treated badly when we take the ship in. The opposite is true and every man jack of you will be pardoned, whether you supported the mutiny in the first place or not—'

'Rubbish! It's all lies. Give in now and you'll be slaves forever!'

There were murmurs of support for Greybeard from the dissenters, some of whom had gathered behind him, and Anson knew that if he delayed for another moment the tide of support for taking the ship in could disappear.

He seized the moment. 'Master, set fore-topsail! We'll get under way without further ado.'

The master raised his speaking trumpet to relay the order. But before he could do so Greybeard snarled, pushed his way in front of Anson and drew a pistol from his belt, shouting: 'I'll see you die before I let you take this ship in, you government lackey!'

Anson stood, helpless, as the agitator slowly raised the pistol and aimed it at his chest. The thought raced through his brain: so *this* is how I am to die, on the deck of a mutinous ship at the hand not of a Frenchman, but one of our own.

One of Greybeard's supporters yelled: 'Don't piss about – just shoot the bastard right now!'

## 12 - Into Sheer Nasty

Greybeard extended his right arm and raised the pistol again so that it was now pointing directly between Anson's eyes. Then, without taking his own eyes off his intended victim, he reached over with his left hand and cocked the weapon.

It was only a foot away. No-one could miss from there.

Anson stared at the barrel, absurdly trying to see if it was engraved around the muzzle like the Royal Mail weapons. But it was not.

Greybeard, his face full of venom and hatred, paused, savouring the moments before making the kill. But he left pulling the trigger for just a little too long.

His threat had clearly angered some of the loyal seamen and panicked others who knew the officer's death could put nooses around their own necks. There was hostile muttering and one of them shouted: 'Leave him alone. If you kill an officer we'll all be dead men!'

For a split second the world stood still, but then from somewhere to Anson's right a belaying pin came flying through the air. Its point caught the agitator in the neck and he fell back against the taffrail spraying blood from the wound. And, as his arm jolted up, his trigger finger tightened and the pistol went off with a loud crack, the ball flying harmlessly skyward.

Rooted to the spot at such a narrow escape, Anson could only watch as several of the loyal hands closed on the agitator and before he could shout to them to hold him the man tumbled over the side and hit the water. Whether he fell or was pushed, Anson could not – and later would not – tell.

He rushed to the side but the man was floating away on the tide, head down as if already lifeless. As Anson and the rest of those on deck watched, the body turned over and sank slowly, leaving only a few bubbles and a smear of blood on the surface.

Anson watched until the bubbles ceased, then made a conscious effort to pull himself together. The other two delegates were still on board, and however it was achieved he knew they must leave the ship before the disaffected men joined them in causing more trouble.

He grabbed one of the delegates by the shoulder and urged him. 'Either join us in taking the ship in or leave now.'

But the man struggled free shouting: 'Join you? No chance!' and he and his companion backed away. One called to the other malcontents: 'We're leaving and the minute we're gone the rest of the ships will open fire on this floating prison again. If you want your rights and you want to stay alive you'd best join *us* afore it's too late!'

Anson quickly debated with himself whether or not he should call on the bosun and marines to restrain them, clap them in irons and take them in with the ship, but decided against it. If they were taken, he reasoned, the rest of the dissidents would be stirred up and there could be further trouble. No, best let them go and risk coming under fire again. No doubt they would be dealt with appropriately when the mutiny came to an end, as he now felt certain it would.

As the delegates clambered over the side to jeers from some of the loyal hands, a few of their watching sympathisers moved forward to join them, climbing down the side netting into their waiting boat manned by fellow mutineers.

Anson looked down to see them struggling to find room to squat in the thwarts and then the coxswain untied the painter and they shoved off, awkwardly at first until the oarsmen settled into a rhythm.

At his elbow, Sergeant Kennard grunted: 'Good riddance to bad rubbish!' and spat over the side.

It would take the delegates' boat a while to clear the ship, Anson reckoned, and the firing would not re-start until the gun crews aboard the mutinous ships could see that their mates were out of danger, so he had a few minutes to get under way.

He turned to the master. 'As I was saying before we were so rudely interrupted, Mister Sadler, crack on what's left of our canvas! Let's get well under way before they start firing on us again.'

As soon as the delegates' boat was judged far enough away from *Euphemus* the gun crews of what could now be seen to be the mutinous *Director* and *Monmouth* re-opened a brisk fire. But, Anson noted with satisfaction, they were again attempting to cut away the top hamper and not a man had yet been injured.

The mutineers were most certainly doing their damnedest to prevent them from taking the ship in, but were still refusing to endanger fellow seamen.

They were stripping *Euphemus* of some of her rigging and shredding her sails, but with a freshening breeze behind her, she was soon out of range and before long they were reaching safety under the cover of the Sheerness batteries.

Anson vowed to himself that he would never again call the place "Sheer Nasty".

# 13 - A Warm Welcome

The arrival of HMS *Euphemus* in the dockyard, proudly flying the royal standard, was greeted with cheers and genuine warmth from everyone ashore.

Exhausted from their exertions, Anson and his fellow escapers ate their first meal in many hours and grabbed a few hours' sleep.

The admiral himself came on board in the late afternoon and interviewed Anson and the bosun, sergeant of marines, the master and the other senior men in the great cabin.

Anson used the opportunity to praise the men who had initiated the escape, playing down his own part in it.

He did, however, mention that an armed agitator he knew only as Greybeard had tried to prevent their escape, but had been knocked overboard by a belaying pin thrown by some unknown hand and drowned.

'No great loss,' was the admiral's reaction. He asked the loyalists if they knew who Greybeard was, but no-one did. 'He was a stranger, sir,' the bosun volunteered. 'There's been a few like him joining the delegates and going from ship to ship causing trouble. And he weren't no seaman.'

The admiral nodded. 'So whoever dubbed him Greybeard got it about right. Nothing but a damned trouble-maker like the ghastly Caribbean pirate whose nickname he inherited. Grey instead of black, eh? But scum by any name. No doubt he and his kind were largely responsible for talking the men into this wretched mutiny in the first place.'

'There were others, sir?' Anson asked.

'We believe there are a good *many* others like him – radicals and supporters of the French, hell bent on causing trouble and cock-a-hoop at the mutiny and desperate to keep it going. Whatever, there's one less now and good riddance.'

'Aye, sir,' the bosun spoke for the others. 'And we'd like it known, sir, that however Lieutenant Anson may try to hide his light under a bushel, so to speak, our escape is down to him. Without him, well …'

'Thankee, bosun. That'll be noted. There'll be precious few officers coming out of this whole affair with reputations intact or enhanced. It's good to hear there's at least one!'

The admiral thanked them for their services, offered each a glass of rum, and told them: 'The petitions that have been presented will receive their lordships' consideration, but not while a gun is held to their heads.'

None could disagree.

While their glasses were being filled, he added with obvious satisfaction: 'You will I am sure be pleased to hear that *Leopard* has also now broken free, as has *Repulse*.'

There were muttered expressions of relief from the group. They were not alone.

The admiral beamed. 'There can be no doubt that the mutiny is collapsing. As well as *Euphemus* and the other two, I've just heard that a number of other ships' companies in the Nore have now struck the red flag. I can promise you that those who give it up like you will be treated leniently.'

'And what of those who won't give up, sir?' Rook asked.

'Some of the real hotheads who have bullied men into straying from their duty will have to pay for what they have done. Our enemy is not the Admiralty, nor your officers who were put on shore. No, men, our enemy is across the Channel. So let's drink to a reunited navy – and death to the French!'

They raised their glasses and echoed his toast.

\*\*\*\*

The admiral took his leave of them, promising that their own officers, excepting several accused of meting out cruel treatment, would be sent back on board forthwith.

Any remaining trouble-makers would be dispersed to other ships but, he repeated, there would be no punishment given to any member of the ship's company for any alleged offence occurring during the mutiny.

Anson accompanied him ashore and the admiral thanked him warmly for the part he had played. 'It will not be forgotten,' he assured him, 'but your role in it will be kept out of the news-sheets. Any public credit must go to the men themselves. I'm sure you understand why.'

'Indeed, sir. I was expecting no bouquets.'

'But in any event you will now have other, more palatable fish to fry, and I've detailed my flag lieutenant to discover where the devil the store-ship you are supposed to be taking passage in has got to during all this muddle.'

'Thankee, sir. The Mediterranean will seem like paradise after Sheerness and the mudflats!'

They walked back to the commissioner's house noting the relief on every face they met.

Returning the salute of a group of smiling soldiery by raising his hat, the admiral remarked: 'As you can see, Anson, they think it's all over bar the shouting and they are right. All it needed was one ship to break away and now all the rest are beginning to follow like sheep. A sniff of the noose tends to remind men that it makes better sense to be a patriot, I find.'

The flag lieutenant was awaiting them and announced: 'The store-ship that's due to take Lieutenant Anson to the Med broke away from the Nore just before the trouble started, sir—'

'And?'

'Via the telegraph I've discovered that she's now in the Downs anchorage off Deal awaiting a favourable wind.'

The admiral chuckled. 'Then all's well that ends well, eh? You had best get down there post-haste Anson, before I think up another task for you!'

## 14 - Rattus Rattus

The following spring Josiah Parkin was engrossed in dissecting a particularly large toad on the dining room table at Ludden Hall when his coachman Dodson returned from Faversham with provisions, the latest London news-sheets and the mail.

'Letter for you, sir. From foreign parts by the look on it – and a wooden box with your address painted on the lid.'

Parkin looked up expectantly from the unfortunate splayed-out amphibian. 'Jolly good, Dodson. Kindly take it into my study. I'll examine it there over coffee. Inform cook, will you?'

Relaxed in his favourite leather-covered armchair, he took up the letter which was addressed to him in copperplate and stated that the sender was "Lieutenant O. Anson, HMS *Phryne*."

It had been nigh on a year since Anson had convalesced at Ludden Hall and set off on some mission connected with the late mutiny, and Parkin had often wondered what had become of his young guest.

Now he was about to find out. With a tingle of excitement he broke the seal, unfolded the letter and read:

*"My very dear sir,*

*Firstly, allow me to repeat my heartfelt gratitude to you and your household for the kind hospitality extended to me during my sojourn at Ludden Hall when I was struck down with the fever last May. No bounds what would have become of me had you not come to my aid, taken me in and arranged the medical treatment and nursing that allowed me to make a complete recovery. You are truly a Good Samaritan.*

*Secondly, please accept my apologies for my long silence since you left me at Chatham Dockyard gates. However, lengthy silences are the nature of things when one is involved in sailing the high seas. Calls at friendly ports where letters can be left for onward transmission or encounters with home-going ships are rare indeed, and it is only now that I have had the opportunity to send a brief account of my doings since we parted company. In brief, it is as follows:*

*The unrest in the ships stationed in the Nore anchorage had reached a critical point when I arrived in Sheerness and I was able to play some very small part in helping to restore the status quo. In truth, the great majority of the men had not wished to mutiny, but their genuine grievances had been used by radical firebrands, both within and without the service, to provoke them into disobeying their officers. Once their fingers were in the mangle it was difficult to extract them, but when the rabble-rousers proposed blockading London or defecting to the French the mutiny quickly collapsed, thanks to brave souls who took the lead in hauling down the red flags and brought their ships back into the paths of duty.*

*But enough of all that. I was then able to join a store-ship under contract to carry salt beef and pork in casks, biscuit, coal and assorted tools etcetera from the victualling yard at Deptford to Gibraltar. After swinging at anchor in the Downs off Deal for some days awaiting a fair wind we endured a painfully slow, immensely boring, but to me restorative voyage to the famous Rock where I was at last able to join my new ship, the 32-gun frigate HMS Phryne, as second lieutenant. She proved a happy ship with a most competent and agreeable captain, George Phillips, a Pembrokeshire man, and I soon became particular friends with John Howard, the first lieutenant, and Lieutenant McKenzie of the marines.*

*At that time our navy had all but abandoned the Mediterranean to the French, that is to say temporarily, but the powers that be had deemed it wise to grant our frigate an independent cruise to annoy the enemy by disrupting his trade along the northern shores of the inland sea. At this we were most successful, appearing where least suspected to snatch merchantmen and taking them in to Gibraltar as prizes to our great satisfaction.*

*In the matter of antiquarian and natural history, I regret to say that although the Mediterranean is a wonderful storehouse, sadly my duties during this hectic cruise have prevented me from enjoying such pursuits to the full. Regrettably runs ashore to famous sites of antiquity have not been possible and I have seen only deep blue waters, not Homer's wine-dark sea. Nor have we been able to follow the course taken by Ulysses, or indeed the Argonauts' quest for the Golden Fleece. Our own quest for enemy merchantmen took priority and I was fortunate enough to be given the opportunity to take in a coaster myself with a cargo of leather goods worth a good deal of money. In the light of your banking past, you will be interested to know that we have therefore fared very well indeed with regard to prize money, which I recall you saying is clearly better than government bonds. You might be surprised to learn that the admiral under whose orders we were pockets an eighth without venturing to sea and you will no doubt understand one of the reasons why all sea officers aspire to flag rank.*

*We are currently undergoing repairs at Gibraltar following a skirmish with the enemy and on completion have been ordered to sail for the good old English Channel where we will join the ships blockading French ports.*

*A sloop leaves here today for Portsmouth so we have the opportunity to send mail home. With this brief dispatch outlining my adventures since we parted company I am sending you a stuffed hoopoe, a blue-cheeked bee-eater and a greater short-toed lark acquired from a taxidermist here. He assured me that the skins have been preserved using arsenical soap in the style of the master bird-stuffer Louis Dufresne and should withstand the voyage home.*

*I trust they will interest and amuse you, and, if so, that you will do me the honour of adding them to your collection of antiquarian and natural specimens.*

*You will also oblige me greatly if you would kindly convey my respects to your niece Cassandra, she of the gift of foresight, and my gratitude to Doctor Hawkins, the indefatigable Emily and the others for their great solicitude to me during my convalescence at Ludden Hall.*

*And to you, dear sir, I send my sincere gratitude for all your kindnesses.*

*Yours affectionately*
*Oliver Anson."*
\*\*\*\*

Parkin smiled at his young friend's thoughtful gesture and turned his attention to the wooden box.

'This will need prising open. Fetch a crowbar Dodson!'

The coachman hurried out and returned with the appropriate tool which he forced under the lid to lever it open.

Parkin could not contain his excitement and peered inside. But all he could see was a scattering of feathers, assorted bones and several small glass eyes that appeared to flash at him in the rays of moted sunlight that streamed in through his study windows.

'Appears the birds have flown, sir!' Dodson grunted, unable to suppress a chuckle at his own avian witticism.

Parkin exclaimed: 'What on earth?' Surely Anson would not have sent these worthless scraps as some kind of naval joke akin to barking dogfish, hammock ladders and golden rivets?

Then he spotted a circular hole at the bottom corner of the box and called for his magnifying glass. There had evidently been foul play of some kind and he intended to get to the bottom of it.

Dodson handed the glass to him and he peered through it at the mysterious hole. It was edged with clear incisor marks that were familiar to a man like him, long self-schooled in the art of rodent dissection.

They were the unmistakable calling cards of a creature he knew by its scientific name: *Rattus rattus*, alias the black or ship rat.

It was a huge disappointment, but Parkin consoled himself that at the very least the offending rat or rats that had consumed the precious specimens would have suffered severe indigestion, even supposing that the arsenical soap had not proved fatal ...

# Historical Note

The 1797 mutinies at Spithead and the Nore came as a considerable shock to a nation that had come to rely on the Royal Navy's growing dominance of the seas.

Britain was at war with Revolutionary France and it was to the "Hearts of Oak" – men and ships – that the kingdom looked for its salvation.

The unrest at Spithead was essentially a strike for better pay and conditions, but the Nore mutiny was far more political and dangerous with agitators hell-bent on blockading London or defecting to the French.

A famous Cruikshank cartoon of the time captioned *The Delegates in Council or Beggars on Horseback* depicts a meeting of the supposedly duped seamen's delegates, with opposition politicians alleged to have incited the mutiny hiding with French revolutionaries under the table.

Travel and communications in the late 18th century were primitive by today's high-speed standards. Journeys that now take a few hours could take days on horseback or by coach. And although the navy's shutter telegraph signalling system could convey brief messages from Portsmouth and Chatham to the Admiralty in London and vice versa in minutes, at times of crisis like this it was sometimes necessary to send the full back-up paperwork. Indeed, would-be mutineers refused to accept assurances that literally came "though the air" rather than on paper.

That is the premise for Lieutenant Oliver Anson's exhausting journeys against the clock as the dramas of the mutinies were played out. Between London and Portsmouth he wisely chose the fastest and most reliable means of travel, the Royal Mail coaches which averaged speeds of up to ten miles an hour, some believing that anything above that might cause fainting or even death.

Grateful thanks are due to Tracy-Leon Barham Esquire and Colonel Robert Murfin for their expert advice on the mail coaches and weaponry of the day, and to jazz trombonist Sean Maple for hints on producing a blast from the post horn.

Although, like much of this story, the defection of HMS *Euphemus* from the mutinous fleet at the Nore is fictitious, it closely resembles actual events that led to the collapse of the mutiny. A few of the characters mentioned, including the flag officers at Spithead and the Nore – and of course the mutineer Richard Parker – existed, but their dealings with Anson are of course imagined.

Lieutenant Anson sails again in **The Normandy Privateer**, the opening chapter of which follows here:

## The Normandy Privateer
## Chapter 1

Sparks flew and the screech of tortured metal set teeth on edge. There was a brief respite as armourer's mate Abel Grist raised the cutlass from his grinding wheel and tested the edge with his leathery thumb.

Watching sailors and marines waited expectantly. But Grist shook his head. In his expert opinion, the blade was not yet sharp enough to disembowel a Frenchman. So he pressed the metal to the grindstone and worked the foot-pedal again.

The on-lookers winced as another stream of sparks spewed forth.

There was nothing like a boat action in the offing to encourage all involved to seek a keen edge to bayonets, cutlasses, half pikes and boarding axes. And the horny-handed armourer's mate was happy to oblige them.

But in a wooden-walled frigate, with a magazine full of powder, this was a job for the open deck. Not the best workspace with a strong westerly breeze ruffling Grist's straggly greying hair.

A few more turns and he took his hand from the wheel to brush away a wisp from his eyes and test the blade again.

Finally satisfied, he handed the cutlass to a waiting seaman who accepted it gingerly and ran his own thumb down the blade.

'You reckon 'tis sharp enough then, Abel?'

Grist sneered gap-toothed at the doubter and growled: 'Give it back 'ere.'

Grabbing it, he held one of his own side whiskers – known in the service as buggers' grips – across the blade and snipped it in two with a flick of his wrist.

Then, smirking happily at this proof of his expertise, he handed the cutlass back and told his audience: 'You could shave a dozy mouse with that and the little bleeder wouldn't wake up!'

*

Attached to the squadron blockading the port of Le Havre, the frigate HMS *Phryne* had been firmly under the scrutiny of the admiral for some weeks. So, to avoid the danger of missing an order or summons, the captain had despatched a midshipman assumed guilty of being behind a series of annoying gunroom pranks into the rigging with a glass to keep an eye out for flag signals.

After many an hour of boredom the youngster almost fell from his lofty perch when he spotted the frigate's number being run up, summoning his captain on board the flagship.

George Phillips, captain of *Phryne*, called for his coxswain and his steward hurried him into his best uniform as the barge was being lowered.

A proud Welshman from Pembrokeshire with prematurely iron-grey hair, a florid complexion hinting at his enjoyment of good brandy, and the beginnings of a paunch due to lack of exercise rather than fine dining, he clambered a trifle clumsily down into the boat, nodding to the coxswain who growled: 'Dip oars.'

As he was rowed across through a slight swell, Phillips pondered possible reasons for the summons. Some misdemeanour, missed instruction or perceived laggardly station-holding perhaps? Always possible causes for a dressing-down on blockade duty.

But no, Vice Admiral Sir Ethelbert Leng was no nit-picker. More than likely this would mean orders for a brief detachment to carry out some task or other – normal use of a frigate – and *Phryne* was known for being the speediest in the squadron.

Piped over the side and greeted with all the formality due to a post captain, Phillips was escorted straight to the admiral's extensive quarters, aft on the upper deck.

'Come in, my boy.' Leng gripped his hand warmly and bade him sit. His captains were all 'my boys' to him although he was only a few years older than most of them.

'You'll take a glass of something?' Phillips suspected he needed to keep a clear head for whatever was to come, but welcomed a brandy, telling himself that it would be prudent to sip rather than his usual gulp – and to decline refills if offered.

Perhaps in part because of his diminutive stature and his years of being overlooked in favour of larger boys at school and later as a midshipman, the admiral had applied himself assiduously, climbed the ranks, led like his contemporary Nelson in a number of daring actions – although unlike him had managed to retain all his body parts – and now clearly enjoyed playing head boy at sea.

Small wonder, the one-time schoolboy fag and dogsbody was now God to all in his world, saving only his superiors at the Admiralty. But out of earshot among his fellow officers throughout the navy, his rapid rise and still youthful looks had earned him the affectionate nickname of the Boy Wonder. If he knew of it he no doubt considered it a mite less embarrassing than Ethel, the inevitable nickname of his schooldays for a small weedy boy cruelly christened Ethelbert.

Phillips stole a glance around the admiral's apartment – luxurious and enormous compared to his own not insignificant quarters in the frigate, but then everything in his world appeared miniscule compared to a ship of the line. 'Perhaps one day …' he told himself.

After a few pleasantries and enquiries as to the state of *Phryne*, the admiral got quickly down to brass tacks, as was his wont. He indicated a chart of the Normandy coast laid out on his desk and unclasped his hands to indicate a point that Phillips took to be somewhere to the north.

'I have a task for you, my boy. You're to be let out of school, as it were – off the hook, eh?'

Phillips was relieved. He had been right – there was no misdemeanour to be chastised, but there was a chance to break the monotony of the present service.

Leng took a swig of his brandy and motioned his steward to replenish his visitors' already near empty glass. 'None of us enjoy blockade duty, do we? But just occasionally I get a chance to give one of my frigate boys a few days off …'

'Most grateful, sir. Should I make notes?' The steward approached, rolling slightly with the swell, and somewhat reluctantly Phillips waved away the flat-bottomed decanter.

The admiral appeared not to have noted the abstemious gesture and shook his head. 'Notes? No need. You'll have written orders. Now, draw up your chair and take a closer look at the chart.' They both pulled up closer to the desk and Leng pointed out the small harbour of St Valery-en-Caux nestling in a break in the otherwise sheer Normandy cliffs to the north.

'Caux means chalk, you know,' he explained. 'You only have to see the cliffs to know that there's plenty of it in Normandy. In normal times this St Valery is merely a tin-pot fishing port and boatyard. But, of course, in wartime any usable harbour with repair facilities on the Channel coast has been pressed into military service and is deserving of our attention.'

Phillips nodded. 'I know the coast there, sir. So, may I ask if this St Valery is now of particular interest?'

'It is indeed. As of this very morning I have reliable intelligence indicating that a most troublesome French privateer is lurking there.'

Phillips was all attention. Armed vessels of that kind, owned and officered by private persons, were given commissions, known as letters of marque, from the French government to prey on British merchant shipping. And the Royal Navy regarded them as little better than licensed pirates.

The admiral tapped a document on his desk. 'A royalist sympathiser, already known to us, came on board from a fishing boat at first light with a first-hand report claiming that this particular privateer has been putting to sea once or twice a month with a large crew to cruise off Hampshire, Sussex and Kent intent on seizing small unarmed coastal vessels—'

'What type of vessel is it, sir?'

'We don't know exactly – our royalist friend is a landsman after all. But from what he tells us she's two-masted, mounting up to a dozen guns and well manned.'

'What we might call a gun brig, sir?'

'That's about the size of it. If so, she'll have a shallow draught and won't be too stable in the open sea but'll be fast and manoeuvrable enough to overtake and overwhelm easy prey around the Channel coast.'

Phillips got the picture. Such a raider could fairly easily avoid British men-of-war and a shot from one of her guns across the deck of a coaster would invariably be enough to convince the skipper that immediate surrender was not only wise but inevitable.

The familiar pattern in such cases would be that once the attackers had boarded, anyone who resisted would either be killed or thrown overboard. Those who cooperated would be allowed to make their way ashore by dinghy or makeshift raft.

The fact that the brig was heavily manned meant that a prize crew could be put on board the captured coaster to sail it to one of the Normandy ports, leaving the privateer to continue the hunt. These predators were a menace, deeply damaging to British coastal commerce.

All this was well known to those who had sailed the Channel in these post-revolution years. The admiral did not need to elucidate further.

'Do we know the name of this privateer, sir?'

'We do indeed. She rejoices in the suitably revolutionary name of *Égalité*, and in the past few weeks St Valery's shipwrights, carpenters and riggers have been helping the crew make good some minor storm damage. According to our informer the victuallers are even now busy replenishing her and in a few days she'll be ready for the next foray along the English coast'.

'But you have other plans for her, sir?'

The admiral smiled broadly. 'Indeed I do! And that, my dear boy, is where you and Phryne come in … and I need hardly remind you that if you cut her out successfully there will be a favourable mention in the Gazette – and prize money.'

This time Captain Phillips did not wave the decanter away.

*

Back on board *Phryne*, Phillips called for the master, first lieutenant and lieutenant of marines to outline the mission and formulate plans.

Brandishing his written orders, he told them: 'We're to look into the harbour of St Valery-en-Caux and …' He screwed up his eyes and recited: '... and taking all measures consistent with the safety of your, that is my, ship, destroy or cut out the privateer currently reported to be under repair there … etcetera, utmost despatch … etcetera, etcetera. You get the picture?'

They got the picture – and throughout the day the frigate had headed north and then east along the Normandy coast towards Dieppe.

The opportunity to escape the boring routine of blockade had come as a welcome relief. Every frigate captain – and all those who served under him – aspired to be well out from under the penetrating gaze of the flagship and to be given an opportunity to cruise independently, with a chance of winning glory and capturing prizes. Preferably both.

This was a specific mission rather than a freelance hunting expedition. But, as the admiral had indicated, the possibility of reward was strong.

Once away from the squadron, the captain's sense of freedom was shared by everyone on board, from the quarterdeck to the lowliest newly-pressed landsman.

And although only those the captain had summoned yet knew in any detail where they were bound or why, there was a buzz unknown in the confined atmosphere of blockade duty. For the few members of the ship's company who had ever attended one, it was indeed like being let out of school early.

\*

Night was falling as the ship passed the small fishing town of Étretat, framed by its strange door-like cliff formations – unmistakeable landmarks for mariners.

There was little need for caution. Without her tell-tale white ensign, *Phryne* was instead falsely flying a French tricolour at the masthead – an acceptable *ruse de guerre*.

It was hoped coast-watchers and gunners manning shore batteries would assume the 32-gun frigate to be French, as indeed she was. She had struck her colours two years earlier to a superior British force in the Mediterranean and been duly pressed into King George's service.

In inky darkness just before the end of the middle watch the prevailing westerlies brought Phryne close to her destination.

Men who spent much of their waking hours moaning and muttering about their lot were cheerful enough now. And orders cascaded throughout the ship to prepare for a possible cutting-out raid heightened the level of excitement.

So many seamen volunteered to man the boats that lots had to be drawn. Those who pulled marked wooden chips from a leathern bucket appeared cheerful, if a little thoughtful.

Those whose tokens were blank affected huge disappointment in front of their shipmates, but some were privately relieved – a foray on a hostile, reputedly heavily-defended, shore was a daunting prospect. In any case, all would share the prize money whether or not they were chosen for the boat parties.

Of the men selected, those who could, slept. But by midnight, start of the middle watch, all were wide awake and already preparing for action.

The raiding parties were fed, blackened one another's faces with some hilarity, and confided in their pigtail mates how their possessions were to be disbursed should they fail to return. And for once most had money they had not yet had a chance to waste on strong drink and weak women.

Before joining the Le Havre blockade Phryne had done well for prize money on a cruise along the northern Mediterranean coast, taking several rich French merchantmen and sending them into Gibraltar with prize crews aboard.

The second lieutenant, Oliver Anson, who was to command one of the boats on the raid, had himself taken in a coaster with a cargo of leather goods worth a good deal of money, and before sailing he had drawn 20 guineas of his entitlement in gold from the prize agent on the Rock.

Now, as they sailed along the Normandy coast, he took an old, well-worn uniform jacket from his sea chest and busied himself unstitching some of the seams. The task completed, he secreted guinea and half guinea coins in the gaps in the lining and set about sewing them up again.

It would not make sense to risk damaging his best white-lapelled blue coat, white waistcoat, breeches and stockings on a mission like this; the old jacket and a scruffy pair of trousers better suited to a tramp would suffice.

Lieutenant McKenzie of the marines watched the needlework fascinated, remarking to Anson: 'As a Scot I commend your prudence, but your money will be safe enough on board, y'know.'

Anson grinned. 'Good point. But where I go, it goes.'

'So you are by way of thinking that if the raid goes wrong you'll be able to pay your way home, eh?'

Anson nodded: 'Something like that.'

\*

Captain Phillips had spent the earlier part of the night with the master, somewhat anxiously checking and re-checking the frigate's position. Josiah Tutt, the affable, grizzled senior warrant officer whose job it was to supervise the vessel's pilotage, was an old Channel hand and had already consulted his charts, books and pilot notes.

'What do'you know of this St Valery, Mr Tutt?'

'Well sir, it appears there's tidal streams that run across the entrance at something like two-and-a-half knots on the flood and a little less on the ebb.'

Phillips shrugged. 'That shouldn't trouble our boat crews too much?'

Tutt checked his notes. 'The tidal streams are somewhat complicated on the flood because there's a counter-current, but part of the eddy runs into the harbour. So no, well-oared and heavily laden, our boats shouldn't have a problem. Well, leastways, not with the currents.'

'What about towing the privateer out?'

'That'll have to be on the ebb.'

'And high tide is …?'

The master consulted his tables. 'Just after dawn, sir.'

'Perfect. So if we get our timing right and all goes well, the boats will be able to land the men high up on the slipway and have a little help from the eddy when they row into the harbour?'

'Exactly, sir – and it should help them getting out on the ebb.'

Phillips was satisfied it could be done. 'Capital. Now, master, just make sure the officers and coxswains know about this tidal stuff. Timing will be of the essence.'

He had not needed to spell that out. If the boats were lowered away too early there would be too far to row before dawn. Too late, and they would miss high tide and most certainly be spotted by watchers ashore. And the cutting-out party could only rely on having an hour either side of high tide during which they could be certain there would be sufficient depth to tow the privateer out of the inner harbour.

\*

As the middle watch ended at four o'clock the boat parties were called to the main gun-deck to be briefed on the mission.

Stumbling about in the flickering lantern light they joshed and ribbed one another to break the tension and hide jittery nerves until bosun Taylor's bark silenced them: 'Cap'n present!'

Phillips made his way to one of the 18-pounders, put a foot on the gun carriage and leaned back against the barrel. A lantern swinging nearby lit his face intermittently as he readied himself for the exhortation expected of him.

Every man's eyes were on him and only the slaps of the waves and creaks and squeaks of the ship's timbers broke the silence.

'Well, boys …' He looked slowly around the expectant faces. They were his boys at a moment like this, men on more formal occasions, and lubbers when they got it wrong or when the loneliness of command soured him. 'Yes, my brave boys, at last we've a chance to strike a blow for old England!'

He paused to allow them a ragged cheer and smiled good-naturedly on hearing an unmistakeably fellow-Welshman at the back ask: 'And Wales too, eh sir?'

'Most certainly for Wales, boy. And Scotland and Ireland too!' He knew the Paddies and Scots, who hated being lumped in with the English, would like that.

The buzz of laughter was cut short by the bosun tapping his rattan cane on the cannon and the captain's upheld hand. 'Now this is serious, boys. There's a privateer lurking in the harbour of a place called St Valery—'

'Saint 'oo?' queried a voice from the gloom.

Bosun Taylor banged his cane fiercely and shrilled: 'Hold yer tongue when the cap'n's speaking!'

Phillips smiled benevolently. He knew how to work his audience. 'For the benefit of that man who's obviously spent too much time working the guns and has addled his hearing, the port is Saint Valery …'

His riposte provoked nervous laughter and he paused for effect.

'Yes lads, it's a place called St Valery-en-Caux. That's where we're bound. This poxy privateer's been causing mayhem on our coast, capturing unarmed merchantmen and feeding their crews to the fishes. Now he's holed up and we've a chance to give these cowardly Frogs some of their own medicine.'

He looked round at the sea of expectant faces picked out intermittently by the swinging lantern. 'So, we're going to cut this privateer out. Are you up for it, lads?'

A chorus of muted cheers and 'aye ayes' greeted his call to arms.

And there were more cheers, and louder, when he added: 'If we pull this off there'll be prize money, boys – and likely there'll be lots of it!'

In his case there most certainly would be plenty – thanks to the Admiralty's patently unfair system of doling out the proceeds from the sale of a captured enemy vessel. It would be divided into eighths and then shared out according to rank rather than risk.

Sceptics could well have queried the fairness of a scale dictating that in a case such as this the admiral commanding the fleet would receive an eighth although hundreds of miles away from the shot, smoke, blood and guts. The captain's share was to be two eighths, although in this instance he would be remaining on board the *Phryne*. And a lucky captain could make thousands.

Fair enough that the next ranking officers would share an eighth and the two levels further down the food chain would also each split an eighth.

Less acceptable, in some lower deck eyes, was that the lowliest seaman or marine risking his life on a dicey raid would receive a mere fraction of the rest of the ship's company share of two eighths. Divided so many times over, it was often barely enough for a good run ashore.

But if there were any such sceptics aboard they wisely held their peace in public, saving their muttering for their hammocks.

Phillips was not one for long speeches. 'Now, listen up to the first lieutenant who'll tell you what you're to do, boys. I'd like to be with you, but someone's got to mind the shop while you're enjoying your run ashore ...' He paused to let the nervous laughter subside and added: 'I know you'll do your duty.'

Every member of the cutting-out party knew the captain meant what he said. He had proved himself to them often enough.

They nodded and muttered their assent and Phillips strode away, back to his charts.

*

For Lieutenant John Howard the raid was a golden opportunity, and his eagerness to crack on was infectious.

In allowing him to lead the expedition, the captain of the *Phryne* was doing his first lieutenant a supreme favour. Success could mean an honourable mention in the Gazette and almost instant promotion, not to mention a decent share of the prize money the privateer would fetch once safely alongside in Portsmouth or Chatham.

Certainly failure could mean death, maiming, or kicking his heels as a prisoner of the French until he could be exchanged. But the rare opportunity for advancement outweighed the risks and any naval officer worth his salt would have been eager to lead the raid. Howard, scion of a noble family, was no exception.

Supported by McKenzie of the marines, Lieutenant Anson and young Midshipmen Lampard and Foxe, he briefed the boat parties on what lay ahead.

The three boats would be launched two hours before dawn, and, with extra boarding crews and marines aboard, would be towed nearer the objective. An hour before first light the boats would cast off, slip round the slight headland to the west of St Valery and row hard for the mole – a long, high, man-made stone jetty jutting out into the Channel and sheltering the small natural harbour.

The plan was for the boats to land Howard, McKenzie with his marines and a dozen of the seamen on the slipway at the opening of the inlet used by St Valery's fishermen. The raiders were to deal with any sentries and make their way swiftly down the mole.

Once in the inner harbour, where the privateer was believed to be lurking, it would be down to the marines to take in the name of King George and enable the seamen with them to get on board and prepare for sailing.

Anson and the two midshipmen were to stay with *Phryne's* boats which, after dropping the raiding party on the mole, were to row like hell straight for the privateer, hopefully arriving immediately after she had been taken, and tow her out before the French woke up to what was happening.

Printed in Great Britain
by Amazon